SO-ANE-188

The Mystery in the Old Mansions

Books by Norah Smaridge

The Mystery in the Old Mansions

NORAH SMARIDGE

PROPERTY OF
CUYAHOGA COUNTY
PUBLIC LIBRARY

Illustrated by Robert Handville

DODD, MEAD & COMPANY

NEW YORK

Copyright © 1981 by Norah Smaridge
All rights reserved
No part of this book may be reproduced in any form
without permission in writing from the publisher
Printed in the United States of America

1 2 3 4 5 6 7 8 9 10

Library of Congress Cataloging in Publication Data

Smaridge, Norah.
The mystery in the old mansions.

Summary: Robin becomes involved in a new mystery when
she takes a summer job in a historic house.
[1. Mystery and detective stories] I. Handville,
Robert, ill. II. Title.
PZ7.S6392Mz [Fic] 81-43235
ISBN 0-396-07980-6 AACR2

J

For my friend W. OTIS FITCHETT,
a senior who is young in heart

1

"It sounds like Dullsville," Robin said, handing Aunt Betty's letter back to her mother. *"Me* in that historic house! I hate history and I don't know any dates."

"Then don't go," her mother said. "No one's pushing you to take a job for the rest of the summer. You can stay with Gran until we get back."

"Thanks, but no thanks," Robin said. "Gran's an angel, but I've done all her puzzles. And I wouldn't be able to keep my mind on baking cookies or pulling weeds. I'd be thinking of you and Daddy in Scotland, and me missing all the fun."

"But it won't be a fun trip," Mrs. Green said. "It'll be cold and wet and foggy. Why, there isn't even a movie in the village. You know we're only going so Daddy can sell that piece of land his grandmother left him in her will."

Robin wasn't listening. She sat hugging her knees and seeing pictures in her mind. It was a habit she had. "Bonnie Scotland," she said dreamily. "Oatcakes for breakfast. And bagpipes—not for breakfast, of course. And boys in skirts, showing their bare knees."

"Oh, *Robin,*" her mother said in what Robin called "Mom's dying-duck voice." She put the letter from her sister-in-law on her desk. "Shall I tell Betty you'd like to go to Gatestown to help in the historic house, or not?"

"Tell her thank-you-very-much-I'll-come." Robin jumped up as the doorbell rang. "I'm sorry I've given you and Daddy a hard time. I know it would cost a lot to take me along. But when you remember how mind-broadening travel is —"

"I know, I know," Mrs. Green said quickly. "See who is at the door, Robin."

It was Bunny, Robin's best friend. She was looking pleased with herself. "Hey, Rob. I've got a job!" she said. "Ooops, that's a poem."

"Could be," Robin said. They flopped down on the sofa. "Where's the job?"

"At the new burger place. Sid's Snacks. They don't seem to mind my being fat."

"Of course not. You'll be a good ad for them," Robin said. She was only kidding. Bunny was sweet and fun and she loved her. "It'll be smelly and greasy, but think of the tips you'll get! You may even make enough for a moped." She sighed. "I was going to try there myself but I'm not sixteen yet like you. And Daddy would hit the roof. He's sure I'd fall onto the grill and burn my nose off!"

"He's got a point." Bunny studied Robin's nose thoughtfully. It was small and a tiny bit turned up. "You haven't enough nose to waste. Besides," she warned, "things *do* happen to you, Robin. And always in summer."

"You can say that again." Robin sounded happy about it. "Summer in a murder house last year. And then nearly murdered myself, in England. I haven't been kidnapped yet, though, and there's not much chance of it this summer. I don't see how anything exciting can happen to me in that historic house."

"That's all *you* know," Bunny said darkly.

"There's one in Linfield where the roof fell in last week. It nearly took a girl's head off."

"This one won't. It's been restored, top to bottom. My Aunt Betty—she's young, so she lets me call her Betty—is going to run it for the rest of this summer. It will be open to the public next week for about a month. And about fifteen kids have volunteered to help." She made a face. "I'm going to be one of them."

"They don't know what they're in for with you along." Bunny grinned. "What will the kids have to do?"

Robin thought a minute. "Oh, clean up after the visitors, I guess." This sounded boring, so she went on quickly. "And go around in old-fashioned clothes. You know. Flowered silks with bunchy skirts and long skinny panties peeping out."

"Not the boys, I hope," Bunny said. She eyed Robin's slim figure admiringly. "You'll look lovely, and you'll meet loads of boys. Boys go for historic stuff."

Robin felt cheered. Bunny always found a silver lining. "Maybe it won't be so bad. For a summer job."

Robin's father reacted the way Bunny had when he came home for supper and read the letter from his younger sister. "It looks as if Robin will have to learn some history at last," he said with a smile. "She may even get to like it." He turned to his wife. "And with Betty to keep an eye on her, I don't see what trouble she could get into."

"How about death from boredom?" Robin said coldly.

Her father laughed. "That's one thing you won't die of. By the way, where will you and Betty be staying? In the historic house?"

"Oh, no. In another huge old house close by," Mrs. Green said. "The owners, a very old couple named Gordon, have gone to South America, and Betty is house-sitting for them. She is there already." She frowned. "It seems a lot to take on, even if she gets free rent."

"Betty always manages to get out of paying

rent. House-sitting in a big old house won't bother her."

"Unless the roof falls in," Robin said. "She'd better find out whether that house has been properly restored."

Her parents looked at her blankly. Sometimes they found their only child hard to follow. "Oh, forget it," Robin said quickly. Daddy was such a worrier; she had better not put ideas into his head. "I guess I won't need too many new clothes if I'm going to be wearing old-fashioned stuff."

"At least get some new jeans," her father said. "For off-duty hours. I'm sick of seeing that faded old Gloria Vanderbilt on your rump."

"Hip," Robin corrected. "Unless part of me has slipped." She gave her father a kiss. And, on second thought, her mother too. She wasn't exactly pleased with them for not taking her to Scotland. But, as parents go, they weren't bad. Not bad at all.

2

The shopping trip next day did not take long. They went, as they always did, to Robin's favorite store, Pretty Please. Bunny joined them. She was to start work soon and she wanted to spend her time with Robin while she could.

Mrs. Green tried to hurry them past the perfume counter. "Keep your mind on clothes, Robin," she cried, as Robin began to sprinkle Bunny with a new scent called Summer Dream. "You'll need at least one lady-like dress in case you're invited anywhere with Betty. When we've found it, I'll leave you to choose a couple of blouses." She turned to Bunny. "But Bunny, dear, don't let Robin buy any of those T-shirts with 'See You Later' on them."

Robin laughed. "It wasn't 'See You Later.' It was 'Escape Me Never,'" she told Bunny. "It tickled Daddy but Mom hated it. One day I dropped it on the closet floor and she pretended she thought it was a dustcloth—and *used* it."

They followed Mrs. Green to the Teen Corner, where Robin turned up her nose at a rack of pastel-colored dresses. "Why no black?" she asked. She winked at Bunny. "I was thinking of something in black crepe."

"Then you'll have to go on thinking," Mrs. Green said. She smiled at Miss Cash, the saleswoman, who was watching Robin, amused. "My daughter's been asking for black as long as I can remember. It's a wonder she didn't yell for a black diaper when she was a baby!"

The saleswoman laughed. She knew Robin. "Would you settle for pink plum?" she asked. "It's the latest color." She took a sleeveless dress off the rack and held it up against Robin. "It's really striking with your blonde hair!" She smiled at Mrs. Green. "And dressy, but not *too* dressy."

"It's charming," Robin's mother said, admiring the stand-up collar and the tiny tucks. "What do you think, dear?"

"It's not bad," Robin said. She took the dress and pulled Bunny by the arm. "I'll try it on while you're looking at some others."

"Not bad!" Bunny echoed as they went into the dressing room. "It's super! If I weren't such a fat frump, I'd grab it for myself."

"You're not a fat frump. You're just nice and—pillowy," Robin said. She peeled off her jeans and Bunny zipped her into the pink plum dress. "I loved this dress at sight but it's best not to go overboard about anything with Mom. Last winter I told her I was crazy about a wool cap she picked up at a garage sale. She couldn't wait to tell Gran!"

"What's so bad about that?"

"Gran was just into knitting, that's what. She was taking a course at the Adult School and she made me five hats. Out of terrible odds and ends of wool. She dropped stitches and made *lumps.*" Robin laughed, remembering. "I had to wear them because I didn't want to hurt her feelings."

Bunny laughed too. "I remember the orange and pink one. It looked like a large mop.

17

Dave Wilson said he felt like turning you up-side down and sweeping the floor with you."

"That clown," Robin said. But she smiled.

The dress fitted beautifully. "I'll tell Mom it's okay. Then we can go to the library and come back for sweaters later," Robin said.

"The library?" Bunny squeaked. "What for? You know you never go to the library. I've often wondered how you manage to get such good grades."

"Maybe I'm just naturally bright," Robin said hopefully. "But as a matter of fact, I read loads of books. I'm working my way through that book wall in Daddy's den." She added, "I do most of my reading in bed, with potato chips."

Later, as they headed up Main Street, she explained why she wanted to visit the library. "They may have some books on historic houses. I want to look up the Frost House."

"And amaze your aunt with your knowl-edge," Bunny said wisely. They entered the pretty, red-brick building that was the town library and she led Robin to a desk where a young woman was stamping books. "I'll ask Miss Harper to help you. Librarians are wonderful at helping."

Miss Harper kept nodding her head as Robin described her summer job. "How clever of you to find something so out-of-the-way," she said. "Such a change from baby-sitting or waiting on tables." She got up and looked for an empty table in the Young Adult section. "You girls grab a couple of chairs and I'll get you some books. We have a fine collection on historic houses."

Before long she was back with an armful of books. She dumped them on the table. "I suggest you divide these between you and go through them until you find the Frost House. If it's halfway famous, it should be here somewhere."

Robin pulled some of the books toward her and looked at the titles. *Homes of the Eighteenth Century, Wayside Inns of New Jersey and Pennsylvania, Haunted Houses, Historic*

Inns and Shrines. "Wow," she said, "this looks like work."

"Then get going," Bunny advised, running her finger down an index page. She worked steadily, but Robin soon got sidetracked. "Listen to these crazy names," she whispered loudly. "Jockey Hollow. Spooky Golf Course. Jenny Jump. Let's go and see them when you get your moped."

It was Bunny who found the Frost House. "Got it!" she said. "Page twenty-eight." She flipped the pages. "There's a picture and a lot of stuff about the house. It's stately looking, and very big."

"Here, let me see. Who's going to slave in it, anyway!" Robin reached for the book, but Bunny held on. "I'll tell you what. You take it out on your library card and we'll go home and read it. With a snack."

As Bunny let go, Robin noticed a piece of paper sticking out of the book. She pulled it out and stared at it, her eyes widening. The same name and town, each time in slightly different writing, were repeated again and again. She handed it to Bunny.

Bunny read it and frowned. "Jason Paul Carver. Gatestown," she said slowly. "Isn't that where you're going? Where the Frost House is? Maybe you'll run into him. He certainly has an impressive name."

"He may be a hundred years old. And anyway, that's not his name."

"Of course it's his name," Bunny said, staring at it. "Why would he be writing somebody's else's name? He's probably practicing cal—cal—"

"Calligraphy. The art of beautiful writing," Robin said. "Gran took calligraphy when she got sick of knitting caps. But when you practice calligraphy, you have to use a special pen—this was obviously just a ball-point."

"So?"

"So whoever he is, I'll bet he's a crook. He's probably practicing writing this Jason's name for some dark purpose," Robin said sternly.

21

They were still staring at the paper when Miss Harper came up. "Still at it?" She smiled. "Did you find the Frost House?"

"Oh, yes, thank you," Robin said. "And we found this in the book." She held up the paper. "Someone may want it."

Miss Harper took it and looked at it, frowning. "That must be the boy who comes here sometimes to do research. I think he told Mrs. Benson that his name was Carver."

"What does he look like?" Both girls spoke at once and Miss Harper laughed. "Oh, you'd like his looks. He's dark, strong, with—well, rather strange eyes. But he isn't very friendly. He's always alone, and if we offer to help, he looks upset and leaves. An unusual boy," she said, folding the paper absently. "Really rather odd."

3

The two girls were almost at Robin's home when she pulled a piece of paper out of her pocket. "Look," she said.

Bunny stared. "It's the paper with all the Jasons! I thought you gave it to Miss Harper."

"I did, but she dropped it back on the table. So I decided to keep it."

"What *for?* I guess you're up to something—but what?"

Robin laughed. "I really don't know. But the paper might come in handy if there should be a—well, a forgery trial." She changed the subject fast. "Say, Bunny, will you help me pack? I'm a terrible packer. I never can get the case to shut, and bits of things always stick out."

"I'll do it," Bunny said, good natured as ever. "But you won't need a lot of clothes, will you? You'll be floating around in those stick-out petticoats. But take the new dress. You might run into that Jason."

"Stranger things have happened," Robin said darkly.

On the next day, talk at the breakfast table was gloomy. "I'm not happy about Robin's traveling to Gatestown alone," her father said, frowning. "She's likely to end up in Podunk, Iowa."

"The bus doesn't go to Podunk, Iowa," Robin said coldly. "Anyway, I'm not going to drag you two with me. Or even one of you." She added quickly, in a singsong voice, "I won't talk to strange men. I won't go for a soda and get left behind. I won't get locked in the ladies' room." She smiled at them kindly. "Of course you're welcome to come and see me off. We can have lunch in the bus terminal."

Which is what they did. But just before her bus arrived, Robin gave them one last little poke. "Did you read in the paper about that crazy bus-driver yesterday?" she asked sweetly. "He kidnapped a lot of passengers and drove them into a quarry." Her mother gave a little cry, and Robin bent to kiss her good-bye. "Oh, don't worry about *that.* It's not likely to happen again."

She felt sorry for her parents as they stood there, waving halfheartedly as the bus pulled away. I really shouldn't have said that—especially as it isn't true, she told herself. Daddy'll give Mom a bad time on the way home.

Forgetting them, she put her case on the rack and her book on the seat next to hers. She took a quick look at the other passengers. All old, and all women. Except—she brightened—there was a boy in the front seat, talking to the driver. Nice back-of-the-head, she thought. Nice flat ears. It was funny how some of the best-looking boys she knew had stick-out ears. This one had thick black hair, a change from the dumb blonds at school. He looked very mature, at least seventeen.

Two women sat in the seat behind him. But

perhaps they would get off soon. Robin picked up her book. *Lady Marigold's Madness.* It sounded promising. Mom had chosen another one, by some female they had to read in school. But it had been easy to switch books.

An hour later, the two women left the bus. Robin moved to one of their seats. The boy was deep in a paperback. A spy story, Robin thought. Boys didn't go for romance.

His case was on the rack overhead. A blue case, with bold white initials, J.P.C.

J.P.C.? Robin's eyes widened. Could they possibly stand for Jason P. Carver? Wouldn't that be something?

Maybe it wasn't a J, though. It could be an S. She raised herself partly in her seat, straining forward for a closer look. Her heart began to beat faster. There was no mistake. It was certainly a J.

The boy moved suddenly, and Robin fell back in her seat. He got to his feet, pulled down the case, and twisted around to face her. He pushed the case almost under her nose. "Now maybe you can read without putting your neck out of joint," he said.

Robin went red. He must have been watching out of the corner of his eye. She waved the case away. "You're not very funny, whoever you are," she said. "As a matter of fact, I have a good reason for wanting to know your initials."

He dumped the case on the seat next to him. "Really!" he said.

Robin thought a minute. "But first, tell me if that's your own case, or one you've borrowed."

"It's mine," he said. "If you'll move over, I'll sit next to you. Then you can explain yourself."

Seated, he held out his hand. "I'm Jason P. Carver. And who might you be? You're a little young for a private eye."

Robin flushed with excitement. "You *are* Jason!" she said. "Well, you may like to know that I have a piece of paper with your name

scrawled all over it—as if someone were practicing to forge it."

He looked startled. *"My* name? That's odd.
I certainly didn't write it myself. Not over and
over. I hate my name. I wish I were called
Bob or Tom."

"That's pretty dumb of you, isn't it?" Robin
asked. "With a name like that you're just one
of a mob. Where I live, if you shout 'Bill,' at
least seven boys come running. But Jason is
unusual. It has a—a touch of class."

He didn't seem to be listening. "May I have
a look at that paper?" he asked. She thought
he looked upset.

Robin nodded. "You may, if you'll get my
case down from the rack."

A minute later she was opening her case,
thankful that Bunny had packed for her. It
looked and smelled so nice. Bunny had sprin-
kled a little talcum powder inside. "Because
cases always smell of *shoes,"* she had said.

Robin felt in the pockets. No paper. She
dug in the bottom of the case. Nothing but

shorts. She felt between the layers of clothes, but there was no rustle of paper. "I don't understand it," she said blankly. "It isn't here!"

"It never was," Jason said. "I guess you're some kind of little nut. Girls who try to pick up boys usually are." He laughed, but it was an unfriendly laugh. "I give you credit for thinking up a smart new way."

Robin opened her mouth to say something cutting. But before she could frame it, the bus stopped. Without another word, Jason picked up his case, jumped off the bus, and swung down the lane.

4

Robin slumped back in her seat, angry with herself. After all this trouble, she still didn't know anything more about Jason Paul Carver.

Except that he was good looking, with a nice nose and chin. She didn't know whether his teeth bucked or anything because he hadn't smiled even once.

She pulled her case onto her knees and began to feel through it, carefully. Suddenly her fingers touched a wedge of paper. Bunny had folded the Jason sheet quite small and tucked it into the toe of a shoe!

Too late now, Robin thought, moving it to the zipper compartment of her handbag. She'd keep it with her, though. Some day she might run into Jason again and then she'd stick it right under his nose.

Calming down, she tried to lose herself in *Lady Marigold's Madness.* Maybe she'd learn something about young men. Because Jason certainly seemed to be a young man, rather than just a boy. He had so much self-assurance.

She didn't learn anything helpful. The men in the book seemed to be widowers, and grim. They attracted, yet terrified, their women. At least Jason didn't terrify her.

The rest of the bus ride went quickly. Her aunt was waiting for her at the roadside stop. "Hi, Robin," she said, giving her a hug. "We'll have to make it snappy. I left a strange man back at the house."

"How strange?" Robin asked interestedly. The day was looking promising.

"Oh, he's okay, I guess. A local man. He's fixing a shutter that nearly fell on me." Betty frowned. "Things are always happening in these old houses. Suddenly you find a door locked and the key missing. Or a door unlocked that you left locked. And sometimes the furniture seems to have been moved around!" She laughed uncertainly. "But I'm probably just imagining things."

"Not you—you're too practical," Robin said. "Don't worry. I'll look into it for you."

Betty shook her head. "Better not. You might come up with something. And I mean to stay in this house till the end of the summer."

"Isn't it a huge house for just two old people?" asked Robin.

"Oh, there was a son, Penn Gordon. But he died a few years ago," Betty said. "He was a sculptor and had his studio there."

After a longish walk through a maze of tree-lined roads, they turned into a dead end. A house loomed up through thick trees, not much of it to be seen. They walked up the path to a double front door, which Betty unlocked.

Robin followed her into a wide, shadowy hall. A little light came from small, diamond-shaped windows, some of them in purple glass. It certainly is big, Robin thought, and not very inviting. Maybe she had made a mistake coming here?

Betty pushed open a green felt-covered door that led to pantries and a big kitchen. There was no sign of the strange man. "Gone," Betty said. "Just like that."

"He left me on guard," a voice said. A boy came forward. He had a good-humored face, reddish hair, and a sprinkling of freckles that was somehow attractive.

"Jerry Sands!" Betty laughed and turned to Robin. "I guess the strange man is Jerry's father. And Jerry, by the way, is one of the volunteers." She introduced Robin. "My niece is a volunteer, too, so you'll be seeing something of each other."

"Hi," Jerry said. He gave Robin a quick, approving look. Then he picked up her case. "Tell me where you want this and I'll take it up for you."

"One flight up, the second door on the right," Betty said. "Thanks, Jerry."

Robin went with him up the wide staircase and onto a dim landing. There were doors on both sides, all closed. Jerry opened the sec-

33

ond one grandly, set down the case, and opened the window.

The room was shabby but pleasant, with an old-fashioned wardrobe, two armchairs, and a small writing desk set in the window. Robin admired a yellow pottery bowl and two candlesticks shaped like flowers. "I love these!" she said. "Gran made something like them in her pottery class."

"I guess Caleb West made them—he was quite a famous potter, and a close friend of Penn, the Gordons' son," Jerry told her. "He lived here once but he moved to a crazy barn house in the country. Miles away."

Robin had lost interest in Caleb West. She was looking at the bed, surprised and amused. It was a double bed, with a canopy of heavy yellow satin over it.

Jerry stared at it, his eyebrows raised. "I thought only presidents slept in beds like this. Washington and that lot." He bounced up and down on the bed. "It's comfortable, though. You'll sleep okay."

Robin bounced gently beside him for a minute. "I expect I'll dream," she said. "I'm reading this wild book and I always dream about what I'm reading."

She gave him a quick sketch of *Lady Marigold's Madness,* and Jerry thought it funny. "Sounds like a girls' book—romantic."

"And sentimental," Robin said. "Let's go and see what Betty's doing. Then I'll have to dress up a bit. Betty hasn't got round to filling the refrigerator yet, she told me, so we have to go out to supper." She wished she could ask Betty to invite Jerry to go with them. But she didn't, of course. She didn't want Betty or Jerry to think she was pushy.

5

Betty said they would go to a charming old inn not far away. "Tomorrow we'll cook," she promised, "but tonight I'll treat. You'll love it. Everybody who is anybody has supper at the Lilac Bush on Saturday nights. Even the Carvers—unless they're in Paris or Vienna."

"Carvers?" Robin started. "Do they live here? Is there a boy called Jason?"

"So far as I've heard, the first Carver son is always called Jason." Betty looked at Robin, surprised. "Don't tell me you know any of our local bigshots!"

Robin frowned. "Not *know* exactly. I—er—had a few words with a Jason Carver. Just today. On the bus." I'd better play this down, she thought, or Betty'll think I'm up to something.

"I can't picture a Carver on a bus." Betty sounded amused. "They're said to dash around in tiny foreign cars."

At the Lilac Bush they were settled at a table with a good view of the big dining room. Robin looked around her approvingly. She hoped they would come here every week. The menu was tempting, full of summery things she liked. And the tables were set so prettily, with pastel cloths and pale pink candles in silvery candlesticks.

Betty was still trying to make up her mind what to order when Robin saw two men following the waitress to a shadowy corner table. They sat down and she caught a glimpse of their faces. Her heart beat faster. The candles gave very little light, but surely the younger one was Jason Carver!

She wondered if he had noticed her as they passed. Probably not. He was looking around the room now, but he soon gave all his attention to his companion.

Robin hardly heard what Betty was saying to her. Something about someone named Nott. She was wondering how she could get that paper to Jason. She would like to wave it under his nose, toss it onto his plate—and turn her back on him.

She got her chance after they had finished their main courses, when Betty suddenly said, "Oh, *there's* Mrs. Nott now. I have to speak to her. I'll be back in a moment."

Opening her bag, Robin took the folded paper from the zipper compartment. She would get it to Jason somehow. She couldn't wait to see his face!

The waitress came over with the menu. "Would you like to order dessert?"

"In a minute." Robin smiled at her. "Would you please give this to the young man over there—at the corner table?"

The waitress looked amused. "You mean Mr. Carver?" She hesitated. "Do you want me to wait for a reply?"

"Oh, no, thanks!" Robin said, flushing. "Just leave it beside his plate." She hoped the waitress wouldn't mess things up. She was almost—but not quite—sorry she had started this.

She had a good view of what happened. The older man at the corner table was studying the menu as the waitress bent to the younger one. She said something that made the boy jerk his head up in surprise. Then he stared over at Robin, frowning. He doesn't recognize me, Robin thought. She felt disappointed. He took the paper from the waitress and opened it. He stared at it for a minute, and then looked over at Robin again. She thought he recognized her this time, but he shook his head slowly.

Then he tore the paper into little pieces and handed them to the waitress, saying something that made her smile.

She came back to Robin's table and opened her hand to show the pieces of paper. "He said to give you these," she said. "He also said—er—well, that I should tell you he doesn't understand what this is all about, but he isn't interested."

Robin flushed, furious. He had won—again. He had made it look as if she had sent him some kind of personal note! Suggesting a date or something! She looked up at the waitress. "Well, thank you," she said. She certainly wasn't going to take those pieces. "Would you be kind enough to dump those scraps in a wastebasket?"

Betty came back to her seat at this point and Robin calmed down a little as they ordered their desserts. "We'll spend tomorrow at the Frost House, even though it's Sunday," Betty said. "It won't open to the public for a few days yet. But the volunteers will need to know all the rooms by then. And choose their jobs. Do you want to guide? Or would you rather help in the herb shop?"

"Oh, guide, I think," Robin said. "It sounds like more fun. Besides, I'm terrible at making change."

Their supper finished, they walked back to the house as the last light was fading. Betty had left lamps lit on the ground floor, but they had such dark shades that they didn't help much. Robin wished there was someone in the big old house to greet them, to break the silence. Jerry, for instance, would be nice.

Upstairs, Betty chatted with her as Robin got ready for bed. "If you don't like being alone, you can come in with me," she said. "But I'm such a restless sleeper I might kick you black and blue." Her smile vanished as she made for the door. "I've been here three weeks and should be used to it by now. But it's a spooky sort of place. Stairs creaking. Doors moaning and slamming—that sort of thing."

"Oh, I'll be fine," Robin said. "You can come in to me if you get scared. Leave the light on, will you? I'm going to read for a while."

Actually, she was too sleepy to read more than a few pages. The book soon slipped from her hands, and she lay staring up at the big canopy. Before she knew it, she was dozing—and then fast asleep.

Some time later she woke in the dark with a feeling that she was choking. Someone was pressing cloth over her mouth! She thrashed around, tearing at it—and something gave way. The cloth was still over her face, but it was loose now. She pulled at it and got her head free.

But there still seemed to be something lying on her. She felt fabric, heavy and silky, and pushed at it. When the weight lifted, she rolled over on her side and groped for the bedside lamp.

She turned it on and struggled to a sitting position. Then she saw what had happened. There was nothing over the bed. The heavy satin canopy had fallen on her.

And someone—perhaps herself in her sleep—had managed to entangle her in its clinging folds.

6

When her alarm went off next morning, Robin found it hard to wake up. There's nothing like being smothered, she told herself sleepily. And I don't remember turning off the light.

Getting out of bed, she looked curiously at the canopy. A heap of crumpled satin, it lay on the floor where she had pushed it. There were metal bits in the corners and a funny-looking hook in the center, but she had no idea of how to put it up again. She wasn't sure she wanted to, anyway.

Betty was in the kitchen, fixing scrambled eggs. When she heard what had happened, she looked worried. "The canopy *fell* on you! But I checked it carefully. I simply don't trust anything in this house." She was horrified. "It's so heavy it could have *smothered* you!"

"It nearly did," Robin said cheerfully. "Do you suppose there are any of those funny ghost-things in this house? Evil spirits? They have a German name. Polter—polter—something.

"Poltergeists. Mischievous but not dangerous," Betty said. "I simply don't know. But there's certainly something going on." She sighed. "I guess I shouldn't have invited you here."

"Oh, yes, you should. You saved me from getting bored to death at Gran's," Robin said. "She's a darling, but best in small doses. Besides, you know I love excitement—all kinds. A few polter-things playing silly tricks aren't going to bother me."

Betty looked relieved. "Well, let's leave it at that for now—though I mean to look into that canopy business." She served the scrambled eggs. "We'll have to wait to do the dishes until we come back. We're running late and the volunteers will be at the house before us."

They were—a lively little group, sitting in twos and threes on the elegant flight of steps that led to the front doors of the Frost House. Betty greeted them warmly and checked their names on a list she carried. "Everyone's here—good!" she said. She introduced Robin: "And this is my niece, Robin, who's going to join us."

There were smiles, "Hi's," hands lifted in greeting. Robin spotted Jerry on the top step and gave him a special wave. It was nice to know someone in this crowd of strangers. Otherwise it would feel like the first day of school. They looked friendly, though, except perhaps for a redheaded girl who was checking Robin out from tip to toe. She seemed older than Robin, sixteen or more.

"We'll see first about the clothes you're going to wear," Betty said, unlocking the front door and leading them into a wide, sunlit hall. "You'll find plenty to choose from. We've made a wardrobe room on the next floor, with a dressing room where you can change." She started up the stairs, girls and boys following, and went into a large room that was lined with closets. "After you've chosen, Mrs. Cory, my assistant, will make any alterations you need. But please try to find things that fit."

One of the boys looked into the nearest closet and backed away. "None of this fancy stuff for me," he said. "I'll be working outside, anyway, so I'll be okay in my jeans."

A handsome boy turned excitedly from a closet. "This is my chance and I'm going to grab it!" he cried. "I've always wanted to wear real fancy clothes. Satin breeches and shirts full of ruffles!"

"Then you'll have a field day," Betty said. She raised her voice. "I'll leave some slips of paper on the table here—and some pins. When you've decided what you want to wear, pin your name on it and hang it back in the closet—unless it needs altering. In that case, bring it downstairs to Mrs. Cory." To Robin she said quietly, "Keep an eye on things. I'll go down to the kitchen now. We're hoping to set up the herb shop today."

Robin crossed to a closet, feeling a prickle of excitement. She hoped she could find something really pretty. But not that mud-colored dress. Or this ugly shade of purple.

Ah! She stretched out her hand toward something in a glowing apricot color. It had a tight, low-cut bodice and softly ballooning skirts.

"Not so fast!" A hand touched her arm. "That one's mine."

Robin wheeled round. It was the redhead who had been staring at her so critically before. *"Yours?"* she said. "I thought all this stuff belonged to the house."

The girl smiled and changed her tone. "I shouldn't have said that. Of course it does. But—well, with my red hair, I have to grab the first good color I see. Colors are terribly hard for me. Now, you're a blonde, you can wear anything."

True enough, Robin thought. She never had to worry about colors suiting her. She held out the dress on its hanger. "Okay, it's yours," she said. "It'll look lovely on you!" She turned back to the closet, which was rapidly emptying as girls, squeaking with pleasure, carried away dresses.

The girls had to wait their turn for the dressing room. The boys got in there first. There were cries, laughter, shouts. "Horseplay," Lucinda, the redheaded girl, said. "Why don't they get on with it?"

The boys came out at last, carrying their chosen costumes. Some hung them back in the closet. Others disappeared downstairs. Fred, the good-looking boy, was grinning from ear to ear. "Look what I found!" he said to Robin. "Purple satin breeches and a ruffled pink shirt!"

"You'll look fantastic." Robin laughed, liking him. "Hold that hanger higher, though. You don't want to trip headlong down the stairs."

The green silk dress that Robin had chosen fitted her perfectly. "It might have been made for you," Lucinda said. "What are those bunchy things at the sides—bustles?"

"Bustles sit on your rear, and there's only one per dress," Robin told her. "These things are paniers." At least I've learned something from *Lady Marigold's Madness,* she thought. The heroine in it had a purple silk dress, with paniers.

Robin pinned her name to the green dress and hung it back in the closet. Lucinda, frowning, decided that her dress needed fixing. "Mrs. Cory can nip it in a bit at the waist," she said. "My waist is my best point." And she headed for the stairs.

Robin found Jerry waiting for her on the landing. "Let's explore. We'll head for the top floor and work our way down," he suggested. "There won't be such a crowd that way."

"Good idea," Robin said, staring up at the staircase stretching ahead. "Take a deep breath. These steps seem to go on forever."

She went up easily herself, but Jerry was panting when they reached the top floor. "How do you do it, girl?" he said. "You're not even puffing."

"I'm a jogger from way back," she told him. "Jerry, what's this?" A board was lying on the floor at the top of the stairs. Jerry turned it over. Painted in bold black letters on a white background were the words:

PRIVATE. KEEP OUT.

7

Jerry frowned. "I guess we're too high up."
He looked at his floor plan. Betty had given
each of the volunteers a layout of the house.
"Look at this. We're not supposed to go be-
yond the fourth floor."

Robin considered. "Well, now that we're
here, we might as well have a look around."
She crossed the landing and turned the knob
of one of the doors. "Looks like a maid's
room."

The room was small, simply furnished with
a bed, a chair, a bureau, and an old-fashioned washstand with jug and basin. Robin
made a face. "I bet those poor maids had
to break the ice in their jugs in winter before
they could wash," she said. "No central heat-
ing in those days."

"They probably just skipped washing," Jerry
said. He went over to the window. "Boy, what

a view! You can see all the roofs of Gatestown!"

Robin joined him. The view was mostly of treetops, but roofs jutted out above the branches. "There's the steeple of St. Jude's Church," Jerry said. "And see that red roof? That's where the Carvers used to live."

"The Carvers?" Robin was suddenly interested. "Where do they live now?"

"Oh, they've got a new place about five miles outside town. One of those all-glass houses that make you feel like a goldfish." He added, "They're separated. *She* lives there and *he* lives near where you live. In Ashton." Jerry suddenly lifted his head and listened. "What's that?"

"What's what?" Robin was picturing Mrs. Carver in her glass house. "I don't hear anything."

"Then *listen,*" Jerry said. He moved quietly to the door, Robin following him. For a minute they stood together on the landing.

Sounds seemed to be coming from one of the rooms. Robin moved quickly and put her ear to the door. "You're right, Jerry," she whispered. "There's a fight going on in here—"

"Watch out!" Jerry shouted. The door opened out, knocking Robin off her feet. A boy ran out of the room, clutching something against him. Neither Robin nor Jerry could see his face. He was wearing a nylon windbreaker with a hood, and the hood was pulled up over his head. But they could hear his furious voice. "I'm taking it," he was yelling. "Nobody had a right to give all that stuff away. Some of it should have come down to me."

Just before the boy got to the top of the stairs, his foot hit the painted board, which they had left lying there. He stumbled and fell, sprawling his length. In so doing, he let go of the object he was carrying, a blue bowl. It crashed to pieces on the wooden floor.

The boy picked himself up and stood for a minute, staring down at the pieces. Then he laughed, a hard, mocking laugh. "There goes a fortune!" he said.

Then, slinging his leg over the banister without turning around, he slid down the flight of stairs and was gone.

8

Robin jumped up and rubbed her elbow. Not broken, she thought, but it'll be bruised. I went down with a crash.

She joined Jerry and they looked over the banister and down the stairs. There was no one to be seen.

"The other guy must still be up here," Jerry said. He turned back across the landing and into the room, Robin following. There was nobody there. Large packing cases, closed and labeled, stood around. "Eleven," Robin counted. "One of them has been broken open."

She considered for a moment. "I suppose we'd better go down and tell Betty about this. She'll probably be mad at us for coming to this floor."

"It's a good thing we did," Jerry said. "Somebody's helping himself out of these cases. If we hadn't seen him, nobody would know."

"I didn't see his face," Robin said. "I don't think I'd know him again. Even though—there *was* something familiar about him." She looked puzzled.

They went down the stairs together. At the bottom, Robin paused. "Jerry, will you stay here?" she said. "And see if anyone comes down. I'll get Betty."

She made her way to the kitchen but it was not easy to take Betty aside. Her aunt was busy with three other women, filling and labeling jars of herbs. A delicious fragrance hung over the room.

Robin said to her quietly, "Could I see you for a minute somewhere private? It's important."

Betty's eyebrows rose. "Of course. But we'll have to make it snappy. I seem to be needed everywhere." She led Robin to a pantry off the kitchen and closed the door behind them. "Is there trouble about the clothes? I expect Lucinda is fussing. She's said to be difficult."

"Oh, no, we all got what we wanted. Certainly Lucinda did," Robin said. "But something funny is going on upstairs—on the top floor." She told her aunt what she and Jerry had seen and heard, and Betty stared at her, astonished.

"You only saw one boy. Are you quite sure there were two people?"

"Unless he was having a fight with himself," Robin said. "It wouldn't surprise me. He was acting sort of crazy."

Meeting them at the bottom of the stairs, Jerry reported that he had seen no one come down except a volunteer. So the three of them started for the top floor.

When they reached the end of the stairs, Betty looked around the landing, frowning. "You two shouldn't have been up here, you know. The committee left a board here saying it was private."

"Someone had kicked it aside, and it was upside down," Robin said. "I suppose we shouldn't have poked our noses in, but I thought we could just take a peek at one of the rooms—after the long climb up."

"Now you're here, we'd better have a good look around," Jerry said. "Somebody may still be in the room—" He broke off, staring at the floor. "Say, Robin, all the broken bits have been cleaned up!"

Robin stared too. "Except this," she said, picking up a fragment and handing it to Betty.

Betty turned the piece over gently in her hands. "It looks like part of the beautiful blue bowl that used to stand on the sideboard in the dining room. But what on earth could that boy have wanted with it?"

"Money," Jerry said. "Boy, was he mad when he smashed it. He said 'There goes a fortune!' So I guess he meant to sell it."

Betty nodded. "I don't know about a fortune, but it was certainly a very valuable bowl. Not an antique, though. A famous potter made it, and I believe it's one of a kind." She went with them into the room with the packing cases and frowned at the one that had been broken open. Putting her hand into it, she pulled out some plastic packaging material. "The bowl must have been right here, at the top of the case. Whoever took it knew exactly what it was and what it was worth."

She was so upset that Robin said, "Cheer up." She waved her hand at the cases. "Only one bowl gone—"

"And only after a fight," Jerry said. "What *is* all this stuff, anyway, and where's it going?"

"Art treasures," Betty said. "Mostly antiques, and very valuable. The Frosts were great collectors. They brought things back from all over the world. They kept everything on display here in their home, and some of the things were actually used—for the pleasure of their visitors."

"It's a pity these things are leaving here, then," Robin said. "Now that the house belongs to the town, there'll be more visitors than ever."

"There's still a lot left," Betty said. "Actually, everything was left to the Carvers. They're close relatives of the Frosts. But Mrs. Carver has no great taste for antiques and wanted to leave them to the house. However, that would have meant a full-time security guard. So the committee finally decided to keep enough things for display and to give the rest to the State Museum."

Robin was fidgeting by now, wanting action. "Hadn't we better forget about the collection and look for that second person?" she asked. "Is there any way he could have got out of this room without being seen?"

Betty shook her head. "No. Yes! Wait a minute." She looked around the room and went to a narrow door that was up two shallow steps from the floor. "I've just remembered. One of these doors—this one, I think—opens onto a back staircase."

She had her hand on the knob when the door opened suddenly. A boy came into the room. Tall, dark, self-assured. "I'm sorry. I didn't mean to startle you," he said to Betty, who had let out a cry of surprise. "You're right about this door, of course. It does open onto a back staircase. I've just come up it."

Jason Carver, Robin thought. What on earth is *he* doing here?

The three of them stared at him. Robin exchanged a quick look with Jerry. A look that said, "He's lying! He's been behind that door all the time!"

Jason was smiling at Betty, holding out his hand. "I know you're the young lady who is looking after the house for the summer," he said. "But we haven't met. I'm Jason Carver. My mother decided, after all, that she wanted to keep a blue bowl that Caleb West, the potter, made. So I came to get it." He went over to the open packing case and felt around in it, frowning. "It looks as if I'm too late."

Who does he thinking he's fooling? Robin thought. She looked at him accusingly. "Oh, stop talking nonsense," she said. "You know who took it! And you know who broke it. And you're probably the one who cleaned up the pieces!"

Jason stared back at her, speechless.

"Is that true, Jason?" Betty asked. "Were you up here—with somebody else? And did you both fight—over the blue bowl, perhaps?"

Jason shook his head. "It's a nice idea. Very imaginative. But I've already told you why I'm here." He addressed himself to Betty. "The movers will be taking these cases away tomorrow. I expect you'll be glad to get rid of them."

"I will indeed," Betty said. She looked at her watch. "Well, we haven't solved anything but I have to get back to the volunteers. They've brought lunches and we're going to eat in the herb garden." She smiled at Jason uncertainly. "Perhaps you'd like to join us?"

Robin held her breath. If he came, she would certainly talk to him. Get the truth out of him. Because she didn't believe a word he had said so far. And probably Jerry didn't either.

But Jason shook his head. "I'm sorry, I'd

like to," he said. "But I promised to take a friend to the Lilac Bush." His smile at Betty had a little warmth in it, for a change. "Perhaps you'll ask me some other time?"

They started down the stairs, Betty and Jerry leading the way. Robin followed with Jason, wondering if he would say anything to her on the way down. He didn't. Stealing a sideways look at him, she saw that his face was dark and set.

When they reached the hall, it was deserted. "Good-bye, Jason," Betty said. "Robin, you and Jerry had better head for the herb garden. I'll bring sandwiches for us. But first I must see that the packing case is sealed up again." She went off, and Robin wondered what she was thinking. Surely she couldn't have swallowed Jason's story.

The big front doors stood open, and a girl came running across the hall. It was Lucinda. *"There* you are, Jason!" she called. "Where have you been all this time? I've taken the place apart looking for you."

"Upstairs," Jason said coolly. He gave a

quick, sideways glance at Robin. "I went up by the back staircase. I had an errand to do for Mother."

"You didn't mention *that* before," Lucinda said sharply. "Anyway, I'm starved. Are we going to the Lilac Bush or aren't we?"

Jason crossed the hall to the front door, pushing Lucinda gently aside. "I'm afraid I can't make it now," he said. "But I understand they're serving sandwiches right here—in the herb garden. So why don't you join them?"

9

"Sandwiches," Lucinda said disgustedly. "Who does that Jason think he is!" But she went with Robin and Jerry to the herb garden, helping herself generously from the tray when Betty offered it to her.

The volunteers, finishing their cold drinks, were talking and laughing about the Frost House. "I'm color blind!" one of them cried. "How am I ever going to get those rooms straight? The Orange Room. The Blue Room."

"A seasick yellow room—a pea-soup green room?" There was more nonsense until Betty held up her hand. "I want to thank you all for coming today," she said. "You're free to go now—and on Wednesday we'll open the house to the public. On the table in the hall I've put a little pile of guide books. Please each of you take one home and study it. It will give you the answers to all the questions you'll be asked."

The volunteers left then, and Betty passed the last of the sandwiches to Robin and Jerry. "I'll be staying here until five," she said, "but you two can go on home. Maybe"—she smiled at Robin—"you and Jerry can solve the mystery of the fallen canopy!"

Robin waited until Lucinda left them before bringing up the matter of the canopy. "Say, Jerry, did you loosen that darn canopy in my room—so it would fall down on me in the night?"

Jerry stared at her. "Did I *what?*"

"It was okay earlier, because Betty checked it. But in the middle of the night it fell down and I felt as if hands were stuffing the cloth into my mouth!"

"You mean like a *gag?*" Jerry was horrified. "But that would be murder!"

"Attempted murder," Robin agreed. "But, seriously, I expect I imagined those hands. I was in a deep sleep, and you know how confused you are when you try to wake up." She added quickly, "But I didn't dream that the canopy fell on me. And it was very heavy. I had trouble pushing it off me onto the floor."

"There may have been something in the center that got loose and fell out. I don't know how canopies stay up," Jerry said. "The beds in our house are mostly bunk beds. No tricks with them."

The old house seemed very quiet after the noise and laughter at the Frost House. "Creepy in here, isn't it?" Robin said, staring around the dark hall. "I hate that weird light from the purple-glass panes."

"Like a funeral parlor," Jerry said. "All we need is an organ playing spooky music. And a nice corpse." He stared up at the windows. "There must be a hundred years of grime on that glass. Somebody ought to give the windows a good wash. Let the light in."

"I can think of better things to do," Robin said, leading the way upstairs. "That canopy is still on the floor. I couldn't lift it by myself."

Jerry whistled when he saw it. He went

down on his knees, pulling the heavy satin this way and that. "There are metal bits at the corners, but the central part seems to be missing," he said. He got up, pushing the canopy to one side. "Let's see if we can find anything on the floor."

But there was nothing on the floor, and Robin soon tired of looking. "Now that there are two of us, I feel brave," she said happily. "Let's explore some of the rest of the house. There seem to be a million rooms. But so far all I've been in are Betty's room and mine and the kitchen. And that horrible hall."

They looked at two of the bedrooms on the same floor but found nothing to interest them. "I suppose this is all good old furniture," Robin said, drawing her finger along the top of a bureau. "But it all needs what my Gran calls 'spit and polish.' Mom would have a fit here." They closed the door behind them and went down the stairs to a landing near the bottom. There was a door and Robin knocked before she opened it.

"Ah! This I like!" Robin cried. "A library. A

real library." She added, pleased, "But not a public one."

Of the rooms they had seen, the library was by far the most inviting. Its high ceiling gave an effect of size. So did the row of windows, running above the bookcases that lined the walls. The books glowed in dark colors, and had gold-printed leather bindings.

"And this is a really big desk!" Robin said, sitting down at it. "I think I'll write all my letters here."

"But why do they have everything so dark?" Jerry wanted to know. "Why such heavy drapes at the windows?"

Robin surveyed them. "Oh, libraries ought to be dim. Like churches. You can pull the drapes aside if you want to see better." She started for the windows herself. "What do the windows look out on, I won—" She broke off suddenly, staring at the window.

Jerry paused, his hand on the drapes. "Anything the matter? For a girl who doesn't scare easily, you're a bit jumpy."

"I thought I saw something move behind

the drapes," Robin said, backing away from them. "D'you want to take a look?"

"Anything to oblige," Jerry said. He crossed the room to the fireplace and picked up a poker. "First I'll get me a blunt instrument, just in case."

But though he gave the drapes a few jabs with the poker, nothing happened. No one moved or yelled. Throwing down the poker, he disappeared between the window and the draperies.

Suddenly he gave a cry. "Come on, Robin. There's a door here, and a short passage. Let's see where it goes."

There was just room for the two of them. When they reached the door at the end of the passage, Jerry hesitated, his hand on the knob.

"What are you waiting for?" Robin asked. "It's probably a door to the yard."

But it wasn't. It opened onto a large room.

10

The room, a studio, was huge and bright, with windows giving onto a stretch of grass that ended in a grove of thick trees. "If there *was* someone behind those drapes, he made his getaway down the passage, through this room, and out. Maybe he's lurking in those trees," Jerry said. He turned back into the middle of the room. "This was Penn Gordon's studio. He used to let me watch him when I was a kid. He was a fine sculptor."

"It looks as if someone had been mixing clay in this vat-thing," Robin said. "It can't be Penn, unless he's come back as a ghost!"

"Someone's using the studio," Jerry said. "Secretly, I suspect."

Robin nodded. "I don't blame him. Or her, as the case may be. It's a beautiful studio." She wandered around the room. "Did you ever see so many closets?" She opened one at random. "Look, they're full of what-d'you-call-thems!"

"Busts," Jerry said. "That's what they call head and shoulder sculptures." The busts were arranged neatly on the shelves. They were of people of all ages, some of whom he said he recognized. "Old lady Hooper, a retired schoolteacher. I'd know that nose any-where. And—yes, the minister of the Lutheran church." He added, frowning, "They don't seem very good, though."

"That's why they're here instead of in some gallery," Robin said wisely.

"I don't mean Penn Gordon didn't do good things," Jerry said. "Some of his stuff is in the local historical museum. We went to see it one day from school. Complete with lec-ture." He added, "We can go and have a look if you're interested."

"Some other time," Robin said absently. "Right now I'm wondering what's under *this.*" She was standing at a worktable. On it was a bulky object, wrapped in cloth. "An unfinished bust, do you think?" She touched the wrapping and made a face. "This cloth is *damp.* How come?"

"Sculptors always wrap their work in damp cloth if they leave it unfinished," Jerry said. "It keeps the clay from hardening."

"Otherwise they'd have to dynamite them?" Robin laughed. She wished she could uncover the bust. She even had her hand on the cloth when Jerry said, "Nothing doing! You'd never get it on right again. And we don't want this guy to know we've discovered him, do we?"

"Not yet," Robin agreed. She looked around the studio, put back a bust that she had pulled forward to look at, and closed the closet door. "We'd better leave everything as we found it. After all, I don't have permission to come in here. Though I don't suppose it matters, as I'm staying in the house."

"In spite of canopies falling on you and villains lurking behind the drapes." Jerry's glance was admiring. "How do we get out of here? Shall we go back the way we came, or through the garden?"

"Oh, through the garden. I want to see what's out there."

"Okay. I'll make sure the doors are shut. You go through the garden and meet me in front of the house."

Robin stepped out of the tall French windows. She was wondering whether she ought to tell Betty that she had found the studio windows unlocked. Possibly Betty knew that the studio was being used but hadn't thought to mention it.

Robin forgot about Betty as she stood looking around her. There were no flower beds or smooth lawns out here. Only a strip of grass, leading to thickly massed trees.

She started across the grass, and stopped. Something white was moving among the trees. The sculptor, on his way to the studio? "Whoever you are, come out, come out!" Robin sang. "I won't eat you, I promise."

77

A girl walked slowly out of the trees, brushing at her dress. "Why, Lucinda!" Robin cried. "What are *you* doing here?"

"Oh, it's you, Robin." Lucinda's face was flushed. "I wish you'd stop yelling. What are you doing here, anyway?"

"That's what I asked *you,*" Robin said. "I happen to be staying here, remember. You're not. Are you on your way to the studio?"

Lucinda shook her head. "That's the last place I want to be, believe me. I had enough of that studio when Penn was alive. He was always wanting me to sit for him, and I hated it. But my mother was flattered."

Robin considered. "Well, if you're not going to the studio, where *are* you going?"

Lucinda frowned. "I'm taking the shortcut home—this grove of trees comes out near where I live." She added, coldly, "Satisfied?"

"Not quite," Robin said cheerfully. "But perhaps you'll show me the shortcut. It might come in handy."

Lucinda hesitated, frowning. Then she

shrugged. "Come on, then—but watch out for branches slapping at you."

Following, Robin doubted whether this was really a shortcut. There was no path worn through the grove and the trees were so close together you sometimes had to squeeze through them. Lucinda was picking her way with care.

They came out, at last, onto a side road. "That's my house—up there," Lucinda said, pointing. She looked relieved. "Do you want to go back by the road or the shortcut?"

Robin laughed. "The road. That shortcut of yours needs clearing with an ax!"

"Then go that way," Lucinda said, waving toward a turnoff in the road. "I go straight on." She started off but in a moment she wheeled around. "If you see Jason, tell him I've gone home."

"Jason who?" Robin said, to be provoking. She did not like being ordered about by Lucinda, who couldn't even say "Please."

"Don't pretend you don't know Jason," Lucinda said sharply. "You came down the stairs with him in the Frost House. Remember?"

And she walked on, faster, as Robin started on her way back to the house.

11

Robin was almost at the gate when she saw Jerry coming down the drive. "I have to head for home now," he said when he reached her, "but you'll be okay. There's a big strong guy waiting for you on the steps."

"Not for me," Robin said. "I don't know anyone here except you." And I'm glad I know you, she thought. You're nice, fun, ready to go along with anything.

"Oh, this guy is far more important. He knows everyone and everyone knows him."

"The mailman? The cop on the beat?" Robin suggested. And laughed as Jerry went off, shaking his head.

She saw no one on the drive. But Jerry was right. There was a boy waiting on the steps. A tall, good-looking, self-assured boy.

It was Jason Carver.

Robin smiled at him. Politely, but no more.

She had not forgotten the way he had acted in the Lilac Bush.

His own smile was warmer. "Welcome back," he said. "I was about to give up."

"I expect you want my aunt?"

She had a funny little feeling of disappointment when he nodded. He took an envelope out of his pocket. "Would you give her this, please? From my mother."

Robin took it, wondering what it could be. She gave a little shiver, not from cold, as she unlocked the door with the key Betty had lent her. "Would you like to come in and wait for her? She's due any minute." She smiled nicely at him, wanting to delay him. "You'd be doing me a favor. I don't fancy being alone in this house. Too many things are happening."

"What kind of things?" His tone was sharp. "You're not falling for ghost tales, are you? All these old houses are supposed to have ghosts, but nobody has ever bumped into one."

"Or walked through one, shouldn't you

say?" Robin eyed him rather coldly. "No, I'm not talking about ghosts. I'm talking about canopies that fall on you in the night. And figures lurking behind heavy drapes. And noises . . ."

"That's quite a list," Jason said, frowning. He looked a little worried. "But there must be some sort of explanation. Something quite simple." He followed her into the hall. "I'll stay with you until your aunt comes."

Robin took him into the big sitting room. "The rooms in this house are all so sort of *sad,*" she said. "I can't believe the Gordons really *live* here."

"It was a much happier house when Penn was alive. After he died, the old couple seemed to give up. I think they mostly use the library and their bedrooms."

"The library's fine—and the studio," Robin said, finding him strangely hard to talk with. "Jerry and I discovered the studio this afternoon. That's where we found the windows unlocked—" She broke off as Betty came into the room, looking tired and worried.

"Ah, here you are. I was wondering where you'd got to," her aunt said. She smiled at Jason. "Nice that you have company."

"Robin found me on the steps," Jason said. "I brought a note for you from my mother." As Robin passed the note to Betty, he said rather formally, "Now you're safe, I must be getting along."

On the way down the hall, Robin remembered Lucinda. "I almost forgot. I have a message for you—from Lucinda. She said to tell you she'd gone home."

"Thanks. I'll look in on her there, then. I owe her an apology." His smile was a little twisted. "And a lunch."

At the door he turned suddenly. "I've seen you before somewhere, Robin. But for the life of me I can't remember where!"

"Oh, I'm easy to forget," Robin said lightly. She wasn't going to help him! *"You* must be harder to forget because I've seen *you* before and I remember exactly where."

Jason stared at her. Then he clapped his hand to his head. "Of course," he said. "On the bus. You're the girl on the bus." He smiled at her with sudden warmth. "And you're very pretty. How could I have forgotten?"

Robin laughed. Somehow she couldn't stay mad for long. "You don't want to remember how rude you were to me. It's as simple as that."

"Rude? Was I? Then I apologize," Jason said. "I begin to remember. I was feeling terrible that day. I got on the bus with a head full of worries."

"So you took it out on me," Robin said. "What I thought *really* very rude was the way you tore up the paper with your name on it—when I sent it to you by the waitress. Were you mad because you found I'd been speaking the truth all the time?"

She broke off. Jason was staring at her, looking puzzled.

"Paper?" he said. "What paper are you talking about? And what waitress? And where?"

Robin stared back at him. For a minute she

was speechless. Then she frowned. "You put on quite a good act, Jason," she said. "I told you on the bus that I had a paper with your name written on it, over and over. I was going to show it to you—"

"But you couldn't find it. I remember *that.*"

"Well, I found it, and the waitress at the Lilac Bush took it over to you," Robin said. "You simply tore it up and sent the pieces back to me." Her face went red at the memory.

He was shaking his head slowly. "I haven't been to the Lilac Bush in months," he said. "It couldn't have been me."

"Then who?" Robin asked.

"Who indeed?" Jason said. Suddenly he became formal. "I think I know, but I'll have to explain some other time. I have to get home, and I must see Lucinda first. She hates to wait."

And he raised his hand in farewell and went off down the drive.

12

When Robin went back inside, Betty was refolding Mrs. Carver's note. "She wants us for lunch tomorrow," she said, and sighed. "I suppose she has to hear all about the bowl's being smashed. I'll tell her that the committee will look into the matter, the insurance and everything."

Robin wasn't interested in the fate of the blue bowl. She was far more interested in seeing the Carver house. Would Jason have lunch with them? she wondered. And told herself it didn't matter whether he did or not.

She spent Sunday morning dressing, trying out the Summer Rose make-up Bunny had given her, and brushing her hair back into one fat curl. She put on the pink plum dress, which Betty admired. "I wish girls would wear dresses again," she said. "I'm so sick of these pants and slacks and jeans. Though I suppose they're practical."

Mrs. Carver telephoned to say she was sending her car for them. Robin wondered if Jason would be driving it. But he wasn't. The gleaming car arrived with a uniformed driver at the wheel.

They were almost at the highway when Robin spotted Jerry on his bicycle. He stared in at them for a moment, surprised. Then Robin mouthed, "See you later," and he nodded, grinned, and rode on.

Mrs. Carver met them on the redwood walk that ran all along the front of the house. Scarlet flowers flamed in wooden boxes. And at each end of the walk a small fountain splashed.

The house shone in the sunlight. Everything the eye lit on was made of glass. Robin wasn't sure whether she liked it or not. It was certainly very unlike the Gordon house— and the Frost House, too, for that matter.

"We'll sit on the deck at the other side of the house," Mrs. Carver said, after she had greeted them. "It's cooler there, and there's a view of the gardens. They're at their best now."

When they were settled with cold drinks, Betty brought up the matter of the blue bowl. "We simply can't imagine what happened up there on the top floor. But someone wanted that bowl very badly."

"Because of the glaze. It's the only bowl of its kind," Mrs. Carver said. "Weren't you told about the lost glaze?" Betty was staring at her, puzzled. "No, I suppose not. After it was decided to give most of the collection to the State Museum, everything was done in a hurry—so as not to delay the opening of the house to the public. Anyway," she said thoughtfully, "I suppose the secret is only of interest to art people. Potters, especially."

Robin could not let it go at that. "But just what *is* the secret?" she asked. "Can't you tell us? I do so love a mystery!" She was careful not to look at Betty. She was sure her aunt had promised her parents that she would not let Robin get into any adventures for the rest of the summer.

Mrs. Carver seemed amused at Robin's interest. "It's not much of a story. And, as I said before, I hardly think it is of interest to anyone except potters. But perhaps you *are* a potter, Robin? Young people do so many things nowadays."

Robin shook her head. "No, I've never been into pottery. Of course the potters I know back home are only kids. They don't make precious bowls. Just horrid little pots in funny colors, with bumps where they shouldn't be."

A maid appeared and they followed her into the dining room. After they had been served a delicious dish of thin little pancakes stuffed with ham, Mrs. Carver began her story.

"I suppose we could call it the mystery of the lost glaze," she said. "The blue glaze on that bowl—the one that was smashed—was invented by Caleb West, a friend of Penn

Gordon and a famous potter. It seems he was trying different colors and temperatures. And he came up with this wonderful, glowing blue."

"It's not at all like Williamsburg blue," Betty said.

"Oh, no. Williamsburg blue has become very common. Caleb's blue was like nothing that had ever been seen before. The bowl caused a sensation in the art world when it was shown." She sighed. "And now to think that the secret is lost forever."

"But didn't Caleb write down the—the recipe?" Robin asked. "The way women do when they invent a new dish. If Mom makes even a tiny change in one of her recipes—and it comes out well—she always writes it down."

"Oh, yes, Caleb did write the formula down somewhere. And he told his friends about it. He was looking forward to giving the secret to the art world, but he wanted to use it for a few years himself first." She frowned. "The trouble is, no one knows *where* he wrote it down. Some think he may have scribbled it on a piece of paper and stuffed it into a bowl, or whatever was handy, until he was ready to write it down properly. But others think he wrote it in a notebook and gave it to his sculptor friend, Penn Gordon, to keep for him while he went to Europe. The tragedy was that he never came back."

"You mean he disappeared?" Robin asked. The mystery was getting better, she thought.

Mrs. Carver smiled. "Oh, no, he wasn't kidnapped or anything like that. He died in a skiing accident, in Norway. And his friend Penn died soon after him."

"In another accident?" Two accidents in a short time certainly looked strange.

"No, no. Penn died of natural causes. A heart attack. And if you're wondering if anyone searched through Penn's things for the formula, yes, they did."

"But who?" Robin asked thoughtfully. "It would take experts to do a good job. Why,

I've been staying in the Gordon house over a week and I still haven't been in all those rooms!"

Mrs. Carver began to offer second helpings. Then, seeing that Robin was waiting for an answer, she said, "I understand that the Gordons made a search themselves. They went through Penn's desk and drawers."

"That doesn't sound like much of a search!" Robin was astonished. "Penn could have put the formula anywhere—artists do crazy things!"

"Well, the Gordons are very private people, and very old. They wouldn't want strangers turning their home upside down."

"I suppose not," Robin said. "And of course nobody knows for certain if Caleb West gave Penn the formula." She had a sudden thought. "I guess *Caleb's* house was thoroughly searched?"

"Oh, yes, indeed! Caleb's brother, his heir, brought all kinds of experts in. He knew he stood to inherit a small fortune if the formula for the glaze could be found and sold."

Robin said no more on the subject. But she was thinking hard. The formula might well be in the Gordon house. The first thing she would do when they went home was talk to Jerry. He might have some ideas. Then they could make their own search while Betty was out of the house.

Mrs. Carver and Betty were still talking about the Gordons. "I was amazed when I met them," Betty said. "They seemed too frail to be taking this long trip to South America."

"They probably think it's their last chance. They've done a lot of traveling in their time," Mrs. Carver said. "But they were never collectors, like the Frosts."

Robin began to be bored with this chatter. It didn't give her any clues. Except make her more sure than ever that the old people hadn't made a real search. She was glad when they finished eating and went back to the deck. At least she could look out at the gardens. Those pale yellow roses were so

94

lovely, and she would like a close-up of that sundial at the end of the path.

Suddenly she straightened up. There was a boy beside the sundial. She couldn't see him clearly, but he looked like Jason. Of course she didn't mean to run after Jason, but he just might have a clue or two.

She decided to find out. "Isn't that your son Jason down by the sundial, Mrs. Carver?" she asked sweetly. "I met him when he brought your note to Betty."

Mrs. Carver started. She looked off down the path, and shook her head. "No, dear. That's not Jason. He's spending the day with his father."

She didn't say who the boy was. Maybe a gardener's boy.

"Would it be all right if I took a walk around the gardens?" Robin asked. "I'd like to see the sundial close up. Some of them have such quaint sayings on them."

Mrs. Carver hesitated. She gave a quick look across the flower beds. Then she smiled.

"Of course, my dear. And if you see the gardener, ask him to cut some roses for you to take home."

Robin got up and left the deck. But when she reached the sundial, there was nobody there. Whoever he was, the boy had disappeared.

13

When they got back just before three, Robin was pleased to find Jerry waiting for her. "I thought your bigshot luncheon would end about now," he said. "How did you like the glass house?"

"A bit shiny," Robin said. "But Mrs. Carver was very friendly and nice—and she told us about the secret."

"What secret? Or rather, which secret? The Carvers are always having secrets. Divorces, separations, who-gets-the-kids. Stuff like that. Everyone knows the Carver secrets."

"Everyone doesn't know this one. And it's not a Carver secret," Robin told him. "Look, I've got to talk it over with you. Let's go somewhere out of Betty's sight."

She led him down the path that ran along the side of the rambling old house. "We can sit on the grass outside the studio. Near the shortcut."

"Shortcut? I don't know any shortcut."

"Lucinda showed it to me. I forgot to tell you about that! Remember when you shut the doors and I went out the other way? Well, I spotted Lucinda in the trees and she said she was taking the shortcut home."

"Whatever she was taking, it wasn't a shortcut. I've done yard work here for years and I know these grounds." He grinned. "If you cut through those trees you must have got a few scratches."

"I did." Robin was puzzled. "But why do you suppose Lucinda said there was a shortcut?"

"Probably because it was the best excuse she could dream up to explain why she was there. It looks as if she's up to something. We'd better keep an eye on her."

"Okay," Robin agreed. "But I'm much more interested in solving the secret of the blue glaze. You know all about that, surely?"

"Everyone knew, at the time. But that was at least three years ago. Someone has probably found the formula by now."

Robin shook her head. "That's not what Mrs. Carver says. And, as she pointed out, it's not the sort of thing that would interest just anyone."

"I guess you're right." Jerry got up and stretched. "Let's get going then. Where do we start?"

Robin considered. "The studio, I suppose. We'll go the front way and through the library."

The library was cool and dim. Jerry pulled the heavy drapes back and opened the door to the passage. "I wonder why they bothered to hide this little door," Robin said.

"I suppose sculptors don't want people bursting in on them while they're working. And Penn wasn't a very friendly sort." The passage was dark, but Jerry found the light switch.

He had his hand on the knob of the studio door when Robin pulled at his arm. "There's someone in there," she whispered.

Jerry put his ear to the door. "Two some-ones. Sounds like a lovers' quarrel! Wait—one of them's leaving but the other's still there—"

"Well, let's go in, then." Robin forgot to whisper. "Or we'll lose both of them!"

Jerry turned the knob and stepped inside, Robin following. A girl was standing at a worktable. She was humming as she wrapped a piece of sculpture in damp cloth. "At least she's not a ghost," Robin said aloud.

The girl heard her and spun around. It was Lucinda. For a minute she stared from Robin to Jerry, and back again. She seemed surprised but that was all. "Oh, you again, Robin," she said. "Are you following me or something?"

Without waiting for a reply, she turned back to the sculpture. Carefully, as if she knew exactly what she was doing, she covered it. "Now please leave this alone," she said. "Or you'll ruin it."

"You don't have to take that tone," Robin said coldly. "We'll keep hands off—if you'll tell us what it is." Lucinda was certainly cool, she thought. She didn't seem at all upset at being found in the studio.

Lucinda stared at her. "It's me, of course. Who else? When I was a kid, I sat for Penn, as I told you. He fussed about what he called my good bones. And now—well, now it's Jonathan." She nodded toward the window. "You just missed him."

"And who may Jonathan be?" Robin asked. Jerry was leaving all the talking to her.

Lucinda looked bored. "As if you didn't know," she said. "As if everyone didn't know."

"Robin doesn't." Jerry spoke at last. "She's only been in Gatesville a few days. I scarcely know Jonathan myself. He isn't often around."

Robin was getting impatient. "Will one of you please tell me who he is?"

Lucinda looked at Jerry, but again he was silent. So she turned to Robin, seeming more bored than ever. "Jonathan is Jonathan Carver—Jason's brother. He's a year younger but he looks enough like Jason to be his twin."

14

"Jason's *brother?*" Robin stared at Lucinda, wondering whether to believe her. "I didn't even know Jason Carver *had* a brother!" It would explain a lot, she thought, her mind racing. Then *Jonathan* was the boy in the library, the boy who tore up the paper, the boy who smashed the bowl. . . . She would have to sort all this out later.

"The Carvers try to ignore Jon," Lucinda said. "He's given them nothing but worry since he was a kid. Jason looks out for him, though, and tries to stop him from getting into trouble." She glanced at her watch. "I can tell you anything you want to know about Jonathan—but later. I have to go now." She looked at Jerry. "By the way, what are you two doing hanging around the studio?"

Robin went red. Lucinda was really impossible. They had found her where she had no right to be and she didn't turn a hair. "I happen to be living here," Robin said. "It's you and—and Jonathan—who don't belong here. Unless someone told you that you could come here, of course."

"Oh, the Gordons wouldn't mind. They've known Jon since he was a little boy. And Penn was very fond of him. Penn thought he had a real gift for sculpture."

"And has he?" Jerry asked.

"I think so, yes." Lucinda was serious. "But right now he's working on something he wants to keep secret. I'll tell you, but please don't pass it on. He'd *kill* me."

Robin smiled. "Aren't you being a bit dramatic?"

"Could be," Lucinda said. "But Jon can be—well, scary. If he's in one of his dark moods." With a change of tone she went on. "He's entering a sculpture contest. If he wins, he'll get five thousand dollars. Enough to go to Paris to study."

Jerry's eyebrows rose. "Can't his folks send him to Paris? They've got plenty of dough. I should think they'd be glad to get him out of their hair."

"They think he's too young to go alone," Lucinda said. She started for the door but turned around. "Robin, please don't say anything to your aunt." Her tone had changed. "We'll only be here a few more times. I've told Jonathan that I'm through sitting for him after this."

"How long does such a—a piece of sculpture take?" Robin wanted to know.

Lucinda shrugged. "With Jon it takes forever. He's never satisfied. Always starting over."

She left then, and Robin turned to Jerry, smiling. "Well, that's that. I suppose we can keep their secret. They're not harming anyone."

"Just taking up our time," Jerry said. "Now we're rid of Lucinda, let's start the search in Penn's room."

Forgetting all about searching the studio, they retraced their way through the passage and the library and climbed to the third floor.

"What a house!" Robin said as they reached the landing. "The Gordons must have expected to have a whole army of kids."

"And all they got was Penn—and he only lasted for forty years," Jerry said. He opened a door and laughed. "Look! I've hit the jackpot. This has got to be Penn's room."

Robin peered in and joined in the laughter. "It can't be anyone else's," she agreed. "He sure kept a lot of his work here."

"Favorite pieces." Jerry walked around the room, examining the figures with interest. There were busts and small figures and larger figures ranged along the bookcase, the bureau top, the tables. "He sure liked Lucinda."

Robin picked up a small white pitcher with a black pattern from a table. She looked into it hopefully, but it was empty. "As a model," Robin agreed. "But I'll bet she was a little brat."

"She still is, in an older way." Jerry opened a closet door. "Well, let's get down to business. You try the desk."

They hunted in silence until Jerry made a face. "We're on the wrong track. There's nothing in the closets except clothes that should have been given to the Salvation Army."

"And the desk is almost empty. Just some writing paper. No notebook. No address book. Not even a telephone book." She added, "That leaves only the bureau drawers—"

She stopped, as Betty's voice startled her. Her aunt had come into the room unheard. "Robin," she said crossly. "I've been looking everywhere for you. What on earth are you doing?"

Taken by surprise, Robin said nothing. To her relief, Betty smiled. "As if I couldn't guess! You're looking for the lost glaze. Well, forget it. I promised your parents I wouldn't let you get into any trouble here."

"It's not trouble," Robin said meekly. And she followed Betty out of the room—but without making any promises.

15

In the days that followed, there was no chance to go on with the search. The Frost House had been opened to the public, keeping Robin and Jerry busy there all day. And in the evenings, Betty kept a watchful eye on Robin's comings and goings.

"I was never so tired in my life," Robin groaned at the end of her third day as a Pink Room guide. She flopped down on the steps outside the front doors of the Frost House, waiting for Betty to finish locking up. "It's my *feet.*"

"You shouldn't wear crazy heels," Jerry said. "You could get away with low shoes under that long dress."

"Oh, my feet can take it." Robin's face lit up. "And it's worth a bit of pain. It's really fun, being a guide. I feel so smart, answering all those questions."

"Like what?"

"Oh, they're mostly personal. Where did the Frosts come from? How did they make their fortune? How many were there in the family, and what happened to them all? That kind of stuff." Robin grinned. "If I don't know the answers, I just make things up. You should have heard my description of Hiram Frost, the first of the Frosts! I gave him a long beard, curly black hair, and a big tummy!"

Jerry laughed. "I thought visitors would want to know about the paintings. And dates when things happened."

"Marion Brown takes care of that kind of thing. She's a brain. She knows all about paintings and wallpaper and whatnot. And she has every date by heart, from Creation on!"

"Good for Marion," Jerry said. "But meantime we're not getting on with the search. And it's nearly a week since we started."

"Oh, we'll get back to it soon. Next Sunday would be good. Betty goes to church, and that takes all morning. And she has a date with Mrs. Nott in the afternoon. So we'll have the place to ourselves."

"Good. We've nearly finished Penn's room. Where shall we go next?"

"The library," Robin said. "He may have used that big desk."

"But wouldn't the Gordons have looked in that desk for a notebook?" Jerry asked.

"Oh, I guess so. But why are we so sure that Caleb wrote down the formula in a *notebook?* That's only somebody's idea. I like the other idea better—that Caleb scribbled the formula on a bit of paper and stuck it in a handy pot."

"If he did, he must have taken it out again. Everyone seems so sure that he left the formula with Penn. Of course Penn would have put it somewhere safe. Maybe he sealed it in an envelope and put it in his safe deposit box in the bank," Jerry said thoughtfully. "He could have done that without telling anyone."

"That's possible," Robin said. "Except that—well, Penn Gordon was a sculptor. That kind of person doesn't usually think of such businesslike things as safe deposit boxes. Artists are more likely to think of something offbeat." Jerry looked dashed, so she added quickly, "We'll look into it, though. Just as soon as we finish searching the house." Poking around the house is fun, she thought. She was in no hurry to stop.

On the following Sunday, Betty appeared at breakfast dressed for church. "I don't suppose you'd like to go with me?" she asked Robin. "It'd be nice to have company."

"I'll go next Sunday, maybe," Robin said. "Jerry's coming today. We're taking a walk or something."

Betty's eyebrows rose. "I hope the something isn't what I think it is!" But she didn't forbid Robin to search. She just sighed. "Oh, well, I give up. If you must go on a wild goose chase, do be careful, and be sure to leave everything the way you found it."

As soon as Jerry arrived, the two headed for Penn's room and went through the bureau drawers. "Nothing but old shirts," Robin said. "We'll do the library. It'll take forever with all those books."

"Books?" Jerry stared at her. "We're not going to read."

Robin smiled at him. "We sort of agreed that the formula might be on a piece of paper, didn't we? Well, Penn might have hidden it in a book." Before Jerry could say anything, she went on, "I've read lots of stories where people leave important papers in books."

Once in the library, Jerry shook his head. "You don't mean we have to look in all these? It'd take weeks!"

"Well, not the ones on the top shelves. Artistic people like sculptors don't have much patience. He probably stuck it into some very handy book. Maybe one of these on the bottom row."

Jerry took out a book and opened it half-heartedly. "These don't look as if they've ever been read. Whew, what dust!"

"It's a classic," Robin said. "Nobody reads

classics. Except in school, where they make you." She looked quickly through a few books and sneezed as the dust tickled her nose. "What kind of books do you suppose a sculptor would read?"

"Art books. History. For serious reading, that is," Jerry said. "And look—here's a shelf of stuff that really looks read." He pulled some of the books out. "Sea stories. Adventure tales—"

But though they opened dozens of books and raised clouds of dust, there was no sign of any folded paper. "We'll have to clean this room now, or Betty will have a fit," Robin said. She sneezed. "Anyway, I think we're on the wrong track in here. We may have to fall back on your safe deposit box idea."

"We have to go through the studio first," Jerry reminded her. "We forgot to search it that day when we found Lucinda there. After all, it's a likely place. He may have put the formula with his own stuff."

"You mean with his clay and little knives—

or whatever sculptors use?" Robin asked. "It sounds crazy, but I guess Penn *was* a bit crazy. I mean, why make all those busts of Lucinda? *That* was pretty crazy. So maybe he put the formula in some weird place."

"If he ever had it," Jerry said darkly. "We don't even know that for sure." He returned the last book to the shelf. "Let's find a cloth and chase the dust. Then we can go for a soda. All this makes me thirsty."

"Me, too," Robin said. "And it's getting late. We can do the studio next Sunday if we don't get a chance sooner." After all, she thought, I didn't exactly *promise* Betty I'd go to church with her.

16

Hundreds of visitors came to the Frost House in the days that followed. Robin even saw Jonathan there a few times, but she never had a moment to speak to him. Betty was run off her feet, helping in the herb shop and with the cookery demonstrations in the big kitchens. Jerry was sure that the yard boys had the worst job. "People make more mess than dogs," he said. "They drop paper cups, sandwich crusts, pocketbooks—you name it. One woman even lost her baby!"

Robin, in low shoes hidden by her long silk dress, was on her feet all day but didn't mind. "I haven't had so much fun in years," she said. "My tales about everyone in the Frost family are getting wilder and wilder. I'd put them in a book—if only I could spell."

"Do you think it's okay, kidding people?" Jerry asked.

"Oh, sure. They probably don't believe me,

anyway. I always give them a smile. And I start by saying, 'As far as I know . . .' or 'The story goes . . .' "

"I guess they forget all that stuff as soon as they leave," Jerry agreed. "Most visitors don't want information. They're just passing the time, but they feel they ought to sound clever."

But some of the visitors were really interested, Robin found. Erica Lange, a potter from New York City, was one of them. One day she arrived at the Frost House when the doors opened and took her time going through all the rooms. Until she came to the Pink Room, and Robin.

"I suppose you know all about the art objects in this house?" she said. "I need a bit of information."

"If it's about the portraits or the silver, you'd better see Marion," Robin said. "She's the guide over there, talking to a minister."

Miss Lange took no notice of that. "I'm looking for a very beautiful blue vase that used to stand on the sideboard in the dining room," she said. "I can't find it anywhere."

"Blue vase?" Robin repeated, to gain time. She did not know whether she was free to tell anyone about what had happened to the vase. Better not, until she had spoken with Betty. "Could it have been sent to the State Museum?" she asked. "A lot of pieces ended up there."

"Oh, I don't think so." Miss Lange was positive. "I think they would have kept it here. And I've been waiting for a chance to study it closely. You may have heard that the formula for the blue glaze on that vase has been lost?"

Robin nodded. "Yes, I've heard."

"I had a wild idea that by studying the vase I might be able to come up with something like it myself."

This woman wasn't as much fun as the other visitors, Robin thought. So she decided to get rid of her. "Perhaps you ought to talk to my aunt, Miss Green, about the vase—"

She broke off as a young man crossed the room toward them. It was Jason Carver.

Miss Lange appeared to know him. "Why, Jason, hello!" she cried. "I haven't seen any of your family in ages! How is your mother—and Jonathan?"

"Both okay," Jason said. "What brings you here, Erica?"

Miss Lange made a face. "Caleb West's blue vase. What else? I had an idea I might learn something from it—but it seems to have disappeared. This young lady can't tell me anything about it."

"Nor can I," Jason said. He gave Robin a look she did not quite understand. Warning, was it? He smiled at Miss Lange. "Why don't I take you to Miss Green? She can probably tell you something about the vase."

They went off, but in five minutes Jason was back. "I've left her with your aunt," he said. He looked at his watch. "Can you get away for lunch now? I want to talk to you about—a lot of things."

Robin smiled. "If it's information you want,

I have nothing but wild tales about the Frost family. You're welcome to as many as you can stand."

"No, thanks. Some of your wild tales have already reached my ears," Jason said. "Would you have enough time for lunch at the Lilac Bush? I have my car with me."

Robin looked down at her dress. "Like this? Or shall I change?"

"As you are, by all means. You look fine. I'm so sick of girls bouncing around in jeans and cutoffs."

Robin found Betty and told her where she was going. Her aunt's eyebrows rose. "Well, take your time and have fun," she said. But she looked a little doubtful. "Jason's a nice young man but—well, a bit old for you."

Robin laughed. "It's only lunch. He'll drop me when he finds out what a nitwit I am."

But Jason seemed to be proud of her when they entered the Lilac Bush and people stared and smiled at her long silk dress. He chose a corner table, and ordered the same salad that Robin did. "I usually have the chef's salad," she told him. "It saves so much thinking. It has everything in it—ham, cheese, turkey. Who could ask for anything more?" She eyed the big salad bowl happily when it arrived. "It'll take me hours to get through this."

Jason smiled. "You can eat while I'm talking. I want to ask you a—well, a difficult question."

Robin frowned. "I hope I can answer it. If it's dates or paintings, I certainly can't."

"You can answer it," Jason said. "It's about my brother, Jonathan. Does he show up very often at the Frost House?"

Robin considered, surprised. She didn't know what she had expected, but it was certainly not this. "He's in and out," she said. "I've seen him a few times, but only in the distance." Suddenly curious, she asked, "What *does* he come for, anyway?"

Jason went red. "To see what he can pick up, I'm afraid. Have you heard about anything missing recently?"

17

Robin stared at him, not trusting her ears. "I don't think I understand. What kind of things?"

"Anything that would fetch a few bucks." Jason's smile was bitter. "A silver box. A candlestick, maybe."

"You mean he just helps himself? But that would be *stealing.*"

"Not the way Jon looks at it. You see, the Frosts left their whole collection to my family. To keep or to sell, as they saw fit. My parents have no interest in antiques, so they gave everything back to the Frost House. And, as you know, it was decided to keep some of the things and give the rest to the State Museum."

"And Jonathan objected?"

Jason smiled for the first time. "Loud and long! He felt that my parents should have kept the things and handed them down to *us.*

He probably tells himself he's only taking what belongs to him."

"He has a point there," Robin said, trying to be fair. "But why is he so crazy about money? You must both get fat allowances."

"Fat enough," Jason said. "But Jon spends money like water. That paper you found with my name all over it—Jon wanted to sign my name to a traveler's check." His smile was twisted. "He doesn't see anything wrong in a bit of forgery, provided he keeps it in the family! And he wants to get together enough money to go to Paris to study art."

"Then why don't your parents help him? I should think they'd be glad to see him get settled down to something."

"Oh, they'll help when he's old enough. Right now he's not fit to look after himself in a strange country. He's very young for his age. He tries all kinds of crazy things to make a buck."

"Yard work? Odd jobs?"

"Yard work!" Jason found the idea funny.

"Nothing so sensible. Believe it or not, he's still trying to find the lost formula for the blue glaze. That would bring him a small fortune, he thinks."

Robin started. "Does he—does Jonathan have any clues?"

"There aren't any," Jason said promptly. "Either the formula was lost in Caleb's studio or he gave it to Penn and Penn put it somewhere."

Robin's heart sank. No wonder they hadn't found anything, with Jonathan ahead of them. "Where has Jonathan looked, exactly?" she asked, hoping she did not sound too interested.

"Well, he kept going back to Caleb's studio until the house caught fire and was pulled down. Nothing turned up in the rubble. And he's still looking in the Gordon house." Jason laughed suddenly. "He was furious when your aunt took it over! He thought he'd have the house to himself all summer while the Gordons were away. He was going to try to find out whether any of the panels in the library were hiding secret compartments!" He stopped, surprised by Robin's expression. "Anything the matter?"

"I was just—*thinking.*" Robin said. "Do you suppose he'd play tricks on Betty and me to get us out?"

"I'm sure he would. When you told me about things happening in the house—like canopies falling—I spoke to Jon. I told him I'd speak to Father if he did anything else like that. Jon's afraid of Father, so I expect he stopped."

"Yes, he did," Robin said. She was on the point of telling Jason that Jon was using the studio when she remembered her promise to Lucinda. "Well, that's enough about your brother," she said. "Let's talk about something else. You, for instance."

They covered a lot of ground after that. But, nice as Jason was, Robin thought that he wasn't as much fun as Jerry. Jason was a worrier. He worried about college. He worried about his parents' separation. He worried about his brother.

Jerry, on the other hand, had little on his mind but fun.

After lunch, Jason drove Robin to the Frost House and she went back to work. She took a quick walk around the Pink Room. Everything looked the same. Nothing seemed to have disappeared. She didn't know about all the other rooms, of course.

She was wondering how she could find out—perhaps Betty had a list of what was in each room?—when Lucinda came dashing in the door. "Hi, Robin," she said. Then, in a rush of words, "I hear you've been to lunch with Jason."

"Any reason why not?"

"Not really," Lucinda said, but she looked unhappy. "It's just that I always think of Jason as mine. We've been friends ever since we were little kids." She bit her lip. "I don't know what I'd do without Jason."

Robin was puzzled. *"Jason?* But I thought

you were *Jonathan's* friend. You do so much for Jon. All that sitting for the contest, and keeping his secret and everything."

Lucinda shook her head. "You've got it all wrong. Anything I do for Jonathan is for Jason's sake. Jason worries so much about Jon, and Jon's always in trouble." She changed the subject. "I didn't mean to talk about your lunch with Jason—it just popped out. I really came to thank you for keeping our visits to the studio secret. And to tell you that they're almost over. I've told Jon that I'll only give him one more sitting. I've done enough. I've *had* it with sculptors!"

"Has he finished the bust?" Robin felt a sudden sympathy for Jonathan. "It would be a pity if he didn't finish it for the contest."

Lucinda groaned. "He'd like to start the bust all over again, but I think he's beginning to see that I mean what I say." She frowned. "What he'll *do* is another matter. He'll be so mad I'm going to have to keep out of his way!"

18

Robin had a lot to tell Jerry when he took her to the Soda Shoppe that evening. When she described her lunch with Jason, he looked worried. "I guess it's going to be a thing with you two," he said, frowning.

"What do you mean, a *thing?*"

"I mean you won't have any time left for *me.* I can't take you to places like the Lilac Bush. Only dumps like this."

Robin laughed. "I like dumps. The Lilac Bush is quiet and sort of *stiff.*" She went on quickly as Jerry still looked worried, "It was only that Jason wanted to ask me something about his brother. And he told me a lot of stuff about Jon. But it's not going to be a *thing.*"

Jerry smiled at last. "Then you're still stuck with *me!*" He looked so pleased that Robin went pink and took a long drink of her soda.

"I'm beginning to wonder whether it's worth

going on with the search for the formula," she said. "Jon's been looking for ages. He must have covered everywhere."

"Except the secret places he thinks may be hidden behind the panels in the library," Jerry said. "But I don't go for that idea. It's story-book stuff. I'm sure Penn didn't go that far to hide the formula."

"We didn't finish in the studio, remember? It's just possible that Penn put the formula in some easy place. Maybe he wasn't worried about it's being stolen and just kept it with his own tools."

"We'll take a look next Sunday, then."

On the following Sunday afternoon, Robin and Jerry spent over an hour in the studio and found something they had not noticed before. "Say, look!" Jerry cried. "I don't re-member seeing this door."

"There was a table in front of it, with clay stuff. Jon must have moved it in the mean-time," Robin said.

Jerry disappeared through the door, and

Robin followed him. "Penn had quite a setup here!" Jerry said. "All the comforts of home!"

The door led to a tiny bathroom, and a kitchen that was little more than a closet. "Why, he could hole up here for days," Robin said. "Whenever he was working on something important. He could make a snack and not bother about turning up for proper meals."

They looked in the drawers and on the shelves but there was no formula hidden away. The drawers held spoons and forks and Penn's tools. The shelves had a little china.

Robin was soon ready to give up. "Nothing here," she said, "but let's try Penn's room again next Sunday. I keep getting a funny feeling that the formula is there. I've even dreamed about it."

"And where was it—in your dream?"

Robin laughed. "Once it was stuck in a picture frame. And once it was in plain view on the desk, with an ashtray on top of it."

Now, in the studio, Robin hesitated before the cloth-wrapped bust of Lucinda. At last she said, "I'm going to have a look, I don't care what you say. I'll be terribly careful."

"I don't get it. Why do you want to see a bust of Lucinda when you can see the real thing every day at the Frost House?" Jerry said, watching her.

"I want to see if it's any good. Whether Jon has any chance of winning the contest."

"But you're not a judge," Jerry objected. "How could you tell?"

"I can tell if it's *like* her, can't I?" Robin said cheerfully.

Very carefully, she unwrapped the bust and stared at it. "I'd say it's good. *Very good.* What do *you* think?"

Jerry took a long look before Robin re-wrapped the bust. "Couldn't be better. All but the nose. Lucinda's has a little bump on it."

"Maybe she told him to smooth it out," Robin said. "Maybe—" She broke off. "Quick, let's go out the other way. Lucinda and Jon are coming through the garden!"

19

Some days later, Betty called a meeting of the volunteers before they left the Frost House. "You've all been wonderful," she said. "And we've nearly reached mid-season. The committee feels that you deserve a special thank you. So we're having a dance on Saturday night, for you and your friends. You may each invite one or two people."

"A dance *here?*" That was Lucinda. "But there isn't any ballroom."

Betty smiled. "We'll make one. We'll throw open the folding doors between the Pink and Green rooms. That will give us a good dance floor. And the other rooms on the ground floor will be used for sitting and eats and whatever."

"Shall we wear our guide costumes or our own clothes?" someone wanted to know.

"Just as you like," Betty said. "I don't think we'll be able to part Fred from his ruffles!" She saved the best to the last. "Pete Diamond's band will be on hand with the music."

There were *oh's* and *ah's* from everyone except Lucinda, who looked unhappy. "I'm crazy about dancing and I haven't been to a dance for ages," she said. "But I don't think I'll show up. Jason hates dancing, and I'd feel lost without him."

"Oh, he'll come," Robin said. "I'll ask Betty to send him a personal invitation. Maybe she will even telephone him. Jon, too."

Lucinda looked more hopeful. "That might do it," she said. "He'd be too polite to refuse." Cheered, she began to decide what she would wear. "I love my guide costume and it really does something for me. But those skirts! They'll get wrapped around my legs and I'll fall on my face!"

"You're supposed to hold them up gracefully with one lily-white hand," Robin said, grinning. "I'll show you the jacket of a book I'm reading. *Lady Marigold's Madness.* The heroine looks a bit like you and she's forever dancing."

"Yes, show it to me," Lucinda said, pleased. "On the other hand, this would be a good excuse for a new dress."

"I'll wear my newest. The color's called pink plum," Robin told her. "But it's nicer than it sounds. And I can move freely in it, which is good. When I dance, I *dance!*"

When the big night arrived, Betty and Robin were at the Frost House early. Betty asked Robin and Jerry to check the volunteers as they arrived. "We don't want any gate-crashers," she said. "There are some rough kids in the south end of town and they might think of paying us a visit."

But there were no gate-crashers. Robin and Jerry greeted the volunteers and their friends. In the Pink Room, Pete Diamond's band could be heard tuning up.

"That seems to be the lot," Jerry said. "Let's go on in, Robin. They're starting the first number."

"Just a minute—here comes one more," Robin said, as a boy hurried through the front

door. It was Jason, handsome in a white suit.

"Hi, Robin—Jerry," he said, but without a smile. "Have either of you seen Lucinda?"

Robin shook her head. "No, she's not here yet—unless she somehow got in by another door."

"Did you happen to see Jon come in?"

"Jon, yes. He was one of the first to arrive. But he wasn't with Lucinda. He brought a small, dark girl."

"I can't figure out what's happened to Lucinda," Jason said. "I called for her, and her mother said she went out at two and hasn't returned yet."

"At *two?*" Robin was startled. "But that's *ages* ago!"

"That's what I don't understand. Her mother said her things are still laid out on the bed."

"Do you know where she went at two?" Jerry asked. "She might be yakking with someone and not notice the time."

"She went to the drugstore for a lipstick or something," Jason told them.

135

Robin frowned. "But isn't her mother worried sick? My mom would have called the police—and the firemen—and the Boy Scouts!" She wanted to make Jason smile, but he looked more worried than ever.

"It's a bit early for the police," Jerry said. "Lucinda's a grown girl. She could have changed her mind about the dance and—well, taken off to see a friend."

But Jason shook his head. "I've talked to most of her friends. None of them have seen her today. Most of them knew she was going to a dance here."

Robin had been thinking hard. "Give me the names of the friends you haven't called yet and I'll phone them," she said. "You and Jerry go look in all the rooms here. She just might have turned up, though it's funny she wouldn't have waited for you."

The boys left, and Robin telephoned Lucinda's friends but with no luck. None of them, she noticed, seemed surprised that Lucinda's mother was taking her disappearance so lightly. "Luce and her mother have never been very close," one said. "And Luce can be very secretive, even with her friends."

Jason and Jerry came back to report that no one had seen Lucinda anywhere in the Frost House. "I'll try her home again," Jason said. "Then I'll drive around for a while. I may spot her somewhere."

Jerry looked worried. "This is probably a crazy idea but—well, she just might have been knocked down. By a hit-and-run driver." He added, "We'll come along with you, Jason—you'll feel better with company."

But Jason wouldn't let them. "You've already missed some of the dance," he said. "And this will probably turn out to be a lot of fuss about nothing." He started for the door. "I'll let you know the minute I find her."

20

Jerry and Robin danced after that, but Robin's heart was not in it. "I'm sorry, Jerry," she said. "You're a great partner and I'm dancing like a ton of lead."

"You're wondering about Lucinda. Me, too. I think I'll speak to Jon. Jason didn't want to before because Jon was in the middle of a mob of girls."

"Yes, do that. He might know something. He was seeing a lot of Lucinda, remember?"

"More than she liked." Jerry grinned. "But she will have finished sitting for that bust by now."

When the music stopped, Jerry got Jonathan aside. Jon listened, looking puzzled. Then he shook his head and went back to his partner.

"He says he hasn't seen Lucinda for several days and has no idea where she could be," Jerry reported. "Then he asked whether

Jason was very steamed up—but he didn't offer to help."

"After all Jason does for *him!*" said Robin. She thought for a minute. "Do you think we should tell Betty?"

Jerry wasn't sure. "She's got her hands full right now. On the other hand, she might have seen or heard something."

Betty and her helpers were putting the finishing touches to plates of sliced turkey and ham. "How's everything going?" she asked. "Are they all having fun?"

"Everything's fine, and the band's wonderful," Robin told her. "But we haven't danced much. Something came up and we thought we'd better tell you." She added quickly, "It's nothing about the dance."

Betty's smile faded. "Then what is it?"

"It's Lucinda," Jerry said. "Jason's been here in a flap. He called for Lucinda and her mother said she went out at two and hasn't come back yet."

"Her dance dress and everything are

still laid out on the bed," Robin said.

Betty's eyebrows rose. "But Lucinda was quite excited about the dance. She called me yesterday to thank me for inviting Jason!"

"Oh, she meant to come. That's what's so strange," Robin said. "Jason and I have called all her friends around here but no one has seen her today. Jason's gone looking for her—he'll let us know when he finds her."

"Then you two go back to the dance," Betty said. "There's nothing you can do but wait for Jason to call." As they turned away, she caught at Robin's arm. "Robin, promise me you won't go looking! It's getting much too late."

"I won't leave here," Robin said. They had no idea where to look, anyway. She went back to the dance with Jerry and they danced together and with some of the other volunteers.

Robin was glad when Jonathan asked her to dance. She just might get more out of him than Jerry had. But he wasn't helpful. "This is getting boring," he said. "I've told Jerry that I don't know where Lucinda is. Maybe she had a spat with Jason and decided not to come to the dance."

"She didn't have any spat," Robin said. "And Jason's very worried about her."

"He's the worrying type. Always has been," Jonathan said. He grinned at Robin, and she had a sudden strange feeling. He was lying, and enjoying it. He knew something about Lucinda. She was sure of it.

The dance ended at one o'clock without any call from Jason.

After Betty had locked up the Frost House, she and Robin headed for home. "At least the dance was a success," Betty said. "But it's very upsetting about Lucinda. I'll call her mother as soon as we get back, late though it is. She may have heard something by now. I shouldn't think Lucinda would be so thoughtless as to stay away overnight without telling her mother where she is."

But when Betty called, Mrs. Norton had

nothing to tell her. "She's still hoping that Lucinda is staying with some friend—a new friend, perhaps," Betty reported. "She's going to call Lucinda's father early in the morning. He's away on a business trip."

"I hope it's safe to wait so long," Robin said.

Betty looked at the clock. It was after 2:00 A.M. "Well, there's nothing we can do, Robin, so we'd better get some sleep. Don't worry too much. There's probably some simple explanation."

And with that Robin had to be content.

21

To her own surprise, Robin slept well that night. So well that Betty was up before her the next morning. She turned from the stove as Robin came into the kitchen. "Yes, yes," she said. "I've spoken to Lucinda's mother again—and there's still no news."

"Has she called the police?"

"No, but she will later in the day. She wants to reach Lucinda's father first."

Robin sat down to her breakfast but jumped up again. "I think I'll call the Carvers," she said.

Betty pushed her down in her chair. "I think you *won't*. Lucinda's mother doesn't want a fuss made." She added, "I'm not going to church today. There's too much to do here. I'd like you to help me dust and whatnot."

"Sure. But I asked Jerry to come round early."

Betty smiled. "The more the merrier. You two can clean the silver."

Robin sighed. "Okay. Until lunchtime, anyway."

"Until lunchtime," Betty agreed. "But I'm serious, Robin, I don't want you getting mixed up in this disappearance of Lucinda's, or whatever it is."

Robin did not answer. It was best not to make promises.

Jerry arrived soon after nine, and Robin told him about the call to Lucinda's mother. "She doesn't want a fuss made—and neither does Betty," Robin said. "You and I are on kitchen duty until lunchtime." She lowered her voice. "After that we'll do some quiet poking around."

Jerry nodded. "Where do you think we should start?"

"At the drugstore," Robin said promptly. "We can ask if Lucinda came in there alone, and if she met anyone, and stuff like that."

By one o'clock, Betty had had enough of

Robin's restlessness. "Thanks for your help," she said. "You can go amuse yourselves now. But, Robin, remember what I said."

As they went down the drive, Robin told Jerry, "Betty won't let me call the Carvers to speak to Jason. But *you* can."

To her surprise, he refused. "Jason said he'd call us, and he won't thank us for bothering him."

At Dale's Drugstore, Robin let Jerry do the talking. Mr. Dale knew him well. "I can't explain right now, Mr. Dale, but will you answer one or two questions for me?" Jerry asked.

"So long as it's not about drugs!"

"It's about Lucinda Norton. Did she come in here yesterday about two o'clock to buy a lipstick?"

Mr. Dale was surprised by the question. "That she did," he said. "Took her time over it, too. Said it was for a dance last night."

"Was she by herself?" Robin asked.

"Yes, she was. I remember we chatted for a few minutes."

"Did you—er—notice if anyone was waiting for her outside?"

Mr. Dale couldn't say. "I wouldn't know that. I got a phone call as she was leaving."

They were just going out of the store when a young salesclerk came after them. "I heard you asking about Lucinda," she said. "Yes, there was a boy waiting in a car. She drove off with him."

"Wow!" Robin looked at Jerry. "Now we're getting somewhere." She smiled at the girl. "Do you happen to know who the boy was?"

"Sure. That is, I don't know him personally but I know who he is. One of the Carver boys—Jonathan."

Robin gasped. *I knew it,* she thought. *I knew he was lying to me at the dance.*

The girl was curious. "Anything else you'd like to know?"

"No. No, thanks," Robin said. "You've been very helpful." They left then, and she caught at Jerry's arm. "Let's find a phone booth. I'm going to call Jonathan!"

But she was only a minute or two in the phone booth before she came out, frowning. "No luck," she told Jerry. "A maid answered and I asked for Jon. She said he left about eleven to go to his father's."

22

After that the two roamed around, talking things over. "Sunday, and everything closed," Robin said, making a face. "Even the library. We can try there tomorrow, though. Libraries know a lot about people's comings and goings."

"And how about our other business?" Jerry wanted to know. "The missing formula mystery."

Robin laughed. "Oh, I haven't forgotten it. I keep going over it in my mind. But Lucinda's disappearance is more important right now. Shall we go home and see if Betty's heard anything?"

Betty had. "Lucinda's father is on his way home. He wanted the police called in at once. Mrs. Norton says they'll be questioning the volunteers. They seem to think Lucinda's disappearance may have something to do with the dance."

She had just finished speaking when the bell rang. Robin opened the door to a police sergeant, a keen-eyed young man who asked to speak to Betty.

Betty answered his questions. "I'm sorry I can't be of more help. Lucinda said she was coming to the dance, but didn't show. Nor did she telephone to let me know she wasn't coming." She added, "My niece helped Jason Carver call Lucinda's friends." She turned to Robin. "I don't suppose you've anything to add, Robin?"

She looked so sure of this that Robin hated to say anything. But with the law on her doorstep, what could a girl do but tell the truth? "Well, I *do* have one fact," she told the sergeant. She was careful not to look at Betty. "Jerry and I did a—a little snooping. We found that Lucinda left Dale's Drugstore about two o'clock yesterday with Jonathan Carver. In his car."

The sergeant wrote in his notebook. "Did you see them yourself?"

"Oh, no. The salesclerk saw them. She knows them by sight."

The policeman nodded. "I'll talk to her. And is that all you have to tell us?"

"That's all," Robin said. "Do you have any leads?"

The sergeant shook his head. "If I had, I wouldn't be allowed to tell you. But I'll say this much. You may have given us a good lead yourself."

After he left, Betty turned at once to Robin. "You're behaving very badly," she said. "You promised me you would keep out of this!"

Robin went red. "I didn't *promise*. I said I'd be careful, and I *have* been careful. And Jerry's been with me all the time."

"That's right," Jerry said. "All we did was ask a few questions—and at least one answer seems useful."

Betty frowned. "I'd still prefer to have Robin keep out of things. But it seems no use talking. So let's just have one thing clear. If Robin gets into even a little trouble, I'll pack her off to her grandmother's." She left them then, and a minute later they heard her banging around in the kitchen.

Robin drew a long breath. "Let's get out of here until she cools down. We can sit in the yard and read. I'll bring you the sports page from the Sunday paper."

As it turned out, they did very little reading. Several of the volunteers turned up to talk about Lucinda's disappearance. The news was spreading fast, and neighbors, too, stopped by to talk with Betty.

Early in the evening, Jason telephoned. "I didn't call you before because I had nothing at all to tell you," he said. "I'm at my father's in Ashton now. I drove over here late last night to talk to Jon again—but he sticks to his story that he knows nothing. Then, this morning, a funny thing happened. My mother telephoned and told me to bring Jon home. The police want to talk to him."

"The police have been here, too," Robin said. "They would have found out sooner or later, but I'm afraid I'm the one who helped them get on the ball so fast. Jerry and I reported that a salesclerk saw Lucinda drive off with Jonathan from the drugstore."

"He told me about that," Jason said. "He says he dropped her at the end of her road." He turned from the telephone to speak to someone for a minute. Then he said, "We're leaving now, Robin. I'll let you know what happens with the police."

23

Robin did not leave the house that evening. Betty recovered her good temper and invited Jerry to have supper with them. But she made it clear that she expected them to stay in, watch TV, play games.

That wasn't as much fun as playing detective. After Jerry left, Robin went to bed early and finished *Lady Marigold's Madness.* She thought the book had a dull ending and wondered whether she couldn't do better herself.

It was dark when she woke. The dial on her bedside clock said ten after three. Unable to sleep again, she lay wondering about Jon and Lucinda, going over their relationship in her mind. They didn't even like each other, that was clear. All they shared was the bust of Lucinda on which Jon was working.

It must be finished by now. Lucinda had said she was sick to death of posing and would only give Jon one more sitting. And that had been some time ago.

Robin began to wonder about Jon. Had he taken Lucinda's decision meekly, finished the bust, and carried it off to be entered in the contest?

Or—Robin shivered—had he been furious, determined to have more sittings, to do more work.

The last words Lucinda had spoken to her came back to Robin suddenly: "I've no idea how Jon will take it. I think he's beginning to see that I mean what I say. But what he'll *do* is another matter! He'll be so mad I'm going to have to keep out of his way!"

Robin sat bolt upright. Was *that* what Lucinda was doing? Keeping out of Jon's way? When they drove off together from the drugstore, had Jonathan said something that scared her so badly that she'd decided to disappear for a time? The more Robin thought of the idea, the more sense it made.

On the other hand, where did Lucinda *go?*

Robin slid back on the pillow again. This was another lead for the police. There was nothing she could do herself. Betty had put her foot down firmly, and she, Robin, did not want to be packed off to Gran's!

She lay there, thinking, until an idea struck her. There *was* something she could do. She could go down to the studio and see whether the bust was still there. If Jonathan had taken it, that would mean that it was finished and her new idea was no good.

Slipping on her robe and turning on lights as she went, Robin tiptoed past Betty's door and down the stairs. She reached the library and went through the little door of the passage to the studio. She turned on the overhead light.

Her eyes went straight to the worktable and she started. The bust, cloth wrapped, was still there!

Robin stood for a while, wondering who to

tell about her idea that Lucinda was hiding from Jonathan. Should she call the police right now, or wait till morning?

She was still standing there when she heard a sound coming from somewhere across the room. She stiffened, listening. The sound continued, faint and scratching. A mouse, Robin told herself, trying to smile. Or a—a squirrel, maybe.

But it was hard to tell. The walls in the old house were just about soundproof.

She moved across the room and the sound came more clearly. It seemed to be coming from Penn's little kitchen. But what *was* it? Was it *human?* Robin wished Jerry was with her. Or Betty. Or *someone* . . .

Suddenly, clearly, she heard a cry. Yes, someone was in there, someone who wanted out.

The key was in the lock on her side of the door. But first she wanted to know who was in that kitchen. If it wasn't Lucinda, she certainly wouldn't open the door.

But it was Lucinda who answered her call. "Robin! Oh, Robin! For heaven's sake, get me out of here!"

When Robin turned the key, Lucinda almost fell into the room. Her face was white and there were dark smudges under her eyes. "What time is it? And what *day* is it, for that matter?" she asked. "I feel as if I've been in there forever."

Robin pulled up a chair for her. "Who locked you in? Was it Jonathan?"

"Who else?" Lucinda said bitterly. "He told me he'd drive me home from the drugstore. But on the way he begged me to come here for just one more sitting. I must have been mad to agree, but I did. Then, when I went for a glass of water, he locked the door and said he'd be back later! He seems to think he can *make* me sit for him!"

"And did he come back—or just leave you?"

Lucinda laughed shortly. "Oh, he came back—and threw in a bag of food. If you could call it food. Dry bread and horrible cold frankfurters!"

"He must be crazy," Robin said. "How long did he think he could keep you here?" She added, "I've always thought Jonathan had something to do with your disappearance. I even told the police—"

She stopped. One of the French windows was being pushed open. "The trouble with *you,* Robin, is that you're too smart for your own good!" a voice said.

There was a gasp from Robin, a cry from Lucinda. The two girls pressed closer together as a boy came into the room. A boy with a dark, angry face.

It was Jonathan Carver.

24

Jonathan came farther into the room and stood looking at them. "I won't get rough if you're sensible. Both of you." He took a step toward them and Lucinda backed away. "Lucinda, you go into the kitchen. And you, Robin, stay right where you are. When I've got Lucinda locked up, I'll do the same for you." He laughed unpleasantly. "The corner closet, I think. Though it'll be a tight fit."

"You're crazy," Robin said. Her mind was working fast. "Two of us missing! That will *really* start a search. The police are looking for Lucinda already—"

She stopped. He wasn't even listening to her. He was backing Lucinda into the kitchen.

Suddenly Robin had an idea. She moved quickly to the worktable, hoping that the bust of Lucinda would not be too heavy for her to lift.

It wasn't. It was heavy, but she was able

to pick it up and hold it firmly against her chest.

Lucinda was just inside the kitchen door when Robin shouted to Jonathan. "Look, Jonathan. *I have the bust.* Your entry for the contest, remember! And if you don't leave this studio at once, I'm going to hurl it to the ground and smash it to bits."

Jonathan wheeled around. For a minute he stared at her, unbelieving. Then, as he moved toward her, Robin shouted again. "Don't come any closer. Go straight to that window—and *out!*"

When he didn't move, she lifted the bust slowly to eye level. "This is your last chance. I'm going to count five. One—two—"

"You can't . . . you wouldn't . . ." Jonathan said.

"Three—four—" Robin inched the bust higher.

It worked. With a cry, Jonathan made for the window. "Lock it, Lucinda!" Robin yelled.

"I've got to put this thing down carefully!"

"Whew, that was close!" Lucinda said. "He's gone, but let's get out of here!"

Robin set the bust gently on the worktable. "I don't think he'll be back, but you're right. Let's get out of this place. I suppose we'd better wake Betty and call your parents."

Leaving the studio in darkness, they made their way to Robin's room. "You lie down for a minute," Robin said. "It'll take me a little time to wake Betty. I'll have to do it gently."

But Betty was awake, with the lamp lit. "Robin!" she said. "I thought I heard something."

"You did, but don't worry. It was only me, coming back from the studio—with Lucinda."

"Lucinda!" Betty stared at her as if she thought Robin was out of her mind. "Is Lucinda *here?*"

"Jonathan had her locked in that little kitchen off the studio—because he wanted her to sit for him and she told him she

161

wouldn't," Robin said. "Do you want the whole story now, or should Lucinda call her parents first? She's in my room."

"Oh, tell her to call them at once," Betty said, getting out of bed. "They must be in a terrible state by now, poor things."

Robin went after Lucinda and left her in Betty's room to telephone. Meantime, she and Betty went downstairs to the kitchen to fix Lucinda something to eat.

The redheaded girl was a long time joining them. "I hope she hasn't disappeared again," Robin said, half seriously. "Jon has a key to the studio. Penn gave it to him years ago."

But at that minute Lucinda came into the kitchen. "I talked to Daddy and told him they should finish their sleep and then come and pick me up." She gave Robin a look. "And I called Jason. He has his own telephone, so I didn't have to wake anyone else." She sighed. "Poor Jason! He thinks the way you do—he's afraid Jon may really be crazy."

"Did Jon go back home when he left us?"

"He hadn't turned up when I was talking to Jason. He probably drove off to his father's place." Lucinda frowned. "But wherever he is, the police will soon catch up with him."

Betty had been listening. "I'm afraid the police will take a very serious view. When you get down to it, Jonathan is a kidnapper."

"But I don't think they can do very much to him if I don't press charges, or whatever it's called," Lucinda said, looking worried. "And I don't think I will—unless Daddy makes me. I'm so sorry for the Carvers, especially Jason. Think of a nice family like that having a son in prison."

"I rather think he won't go to prison," Betty said. "They'll make him take mental tests— and probably go for treatment. He wasn't trying to get money from your family. And he would have let you go when he finished the bust."

"It was a kind of *temporary* kidnapping," Robin said. "But pretty scary for Lucinda."

25

Tired though she was, Robin insisted on going to her job at the Frost House the next day. She also had a lot to tell Jerry, mostly over lunch in the herb garden.

"Too bad I missed that scene in the studio!" Jerry said. "Do you think he meant to get rough?"

"If he did, he didn't get a chance to," Robin said happily. "I would have thrown the bust at him. It's a wonder I didn't drop it, anyway."

Jerry nodded. "If they've offered a reward for Lucinda, you ought to get it."

Robin laughed. "Oh, I wouldn't take it. It's the fun of solving a mystery that I like." Her face lit up. "Which reminds me, we've got to get back to the lost formula case."

"That can wait a day or two. You could do with a bit of rest first."

"Maybe next Sunday," Robin said. "If I'm

still here. Betty has said she'll pack me off to Gran's, remember?"

"That's just talk," Jerry said comfortably. "I'll bet she's proud of you after this."

Robin left the Frost House a little earlier than usual. Jerry was right; she *was* tired. She felt she could sleep for a week.

When she reached the house, the young police sergeant was just turning away from the front door. "Ah, there you are, Miss!" he said, smiling. "So you've got your friend back, safe and sound. I wish all kidnapping cases could be solved so easily."

"Easily?" Robin said indignantly. "I never did so much thinking in my life. And let me tell you, thinking is *tiring."*

The sergeant grinned. "Well, you've got a good head on your shoulders. Maybe you'll think of joining the force—when the time comes."

Robin beamed. "I'd *love* that. But I'm not through high school yet." She made a face. "And then there's college. College?" She paused a moment, then changed the subject. "Am I allowed to ask you what's happened to Jonathan Carver, the kidnapper?"

"He'll be coming in later for questioning, with his lawyer. I can't tell you what will happen." He frowned. "It's a funny sort of case. Kidnapping between friends, you might say. No harm done except a lot of scaring." He held out his hand. "I'll be off now. I just stopped by to thank you for your cooperation."

He was gone before Robin could find words to answer. *Cooperation,* she thought. I like that! Why, I solved the whole case myself!

Things were a little dull in the next few days, except for a wonderful thank-you dinner at the Lilac Bush that Lucinda's parents gave for Robin. "Her father and I will never forget what you did for Lucinda," Mrs. Norton said. "Who knows what that boy might have done. He's really crazy!"

Lucinda's father shook his head. "He may not be crazy in the eyes of the law. But he's certainly not normal. He's wild. Spoiled rotten.

That boy wants what he wants and he doesn't care how he gets it."

Lucinda gave a little smile. "I certainly got a bad scare but I was more mad than anything. Now that I'm safely out of that little kitchen, I can't help feeling a bit sorry for Jon. I can't believe he meant to hurt me. He just wanted to *hold* me there. And he *did* feed me—though not exactly my favorite foods!"

There was much guessing about what would happen to Jonathan. By the end of the week, they knew. Jason, looking less worried than usual, stopped by to tell them. "They made Jon go for a mental examination," he said. "And they found he needs treatment. So he's off to a clinic for—well, until he gets himself straightened out. After that"—he smiled—"I think my parents will send him to Paris, to live with a French family they know and study sculpture. The doctors say that much of his trouble comes from not being able to do what he wants."

Robin remembered the contest. "He worked

so hard on that bust," she said. "It's a pity he won't get a chance to enter it in the contest."

Jason smiled. "Don't worry, I'll see to that. I've promised him and he's really grateful— the first time I've seen Jon grateful for anything!"

Toward the end of the week, Robin changed her job at the Frost House. The rush of visitors was slowing down, and she was running out of wild tales to tell them. So she worked in the herb shop, selling herbs and telling people how to use them—with the help of a library book!

"It's easy, and I get to sit down now and then," she told Jerry. "But I can't *smell* any more. And everything tastes of *basil.*"

"What's basil?" Jerry asked, not really interested. "Whatever it is, you'd better lay off it and get your nose back in order. If your aunt goes to church on Sunday, we'll have a good chance to sniff around in Penn's room."

26

On the following Sunday, with Betty safely outside the house, Robin and Jerry shut themselves up in Penn Gordon's room. "If we don't find the formula today, that's the end of it," Robin said. "I wouldn't even bother with this room again, except for those dreams I had."

They moved slowly around, lifting heavy busts and figures to see whether any paper was hidden under them. They looked through the drawers again and poked around in the closets.

Finally Robin sat down in disgust. "I've had it, Jerry," she said. "No . . . wait a minute!" She jumped up and went over to a table crowded with small figures. "I remember seeing this before and looking inside it, but I didn't really stop to *think* about it. What do you think it *is?*"

"A bit of pottery, of course," Jerry said. "Jug—pitcher?"

"But Penn *wasn't* a potter. He was a sculptor," Robin said. "There's not another bit of pottery in the room!"

"So what? Someone gave it to him. Or he just liked it."

"You think so?" Robin stared at the pitcher. "It looks so—unfinished. The shape's nice, but the pattern is a mess."

Jerry agreed. He looked more closely at the pitcher. "It looks as if the potter wiped his brush on it because he didn't have a rag handy." He broke off. Robin was staring at the pitcher, her eyes wide.

"Jerry, *look*. Look carefully at the pattern!"

Jerry looked, and made a face. "If he didn't wipe his brush on it, he just scrawled on it."

"But isn't this a figure—an eight, I think? And this is a letter—and here's another letter."

"And that's a symbol," Jerry said, pointing. He sounded excited. "The kind that's used in chemistry and stuff." He looked from the pitcher to Robin. "I think I see what you're getting at!"

"It's *Caleb's* pitcher. I *feel* it," Robin said. "I can just see it. When Caleb invented the new formula he didn't have paper handy—so he scrawled it on the nearest thing, this white pitcher!"

Robin's hand began to shake. She set down the pitcher carefully. "How can we find out for sure? We'll have to take it to someone who knows about formulas."

Jerry thought a minute. "The Pottery Barn. George Watson runs it. He sells pottery and gives classes."

"Would it be open on Sunday?"

"Oh, sure! Students go there to fire their pottery in his kilns."

Robin pointed to the pitcher. "You carry it, Jerry. I'm too jumpy! Wouldn't it be terrible if I fell with it!"

"Like Jonathan with the blue bowl," Jerry said. "We can't let that happen twice!"

In ten minutes they were at the Pottery

Barn. The owner was taking a bowl out of the kiln. He set it down carefully. "And what can I do for you?" he asked Jerry. "Do you want that fired?"

"Oh, no," Robin said quickly. "We want you to look at it and tell us what you see."

Mr. Watson looked amused. He took the pitcher so casually that Robin trembled for it. "It's an excellent design. Good pouring spout. Graceful handle."

"But the pattern?"

"What pattern? Oh, you mean this?" He tapped it with his forefinger. "Unfinished. Just a scrawl." He looked more closely at it and smiled. "It doesn't look like a pattern to me. It looks as if the potter dabbed down a telephone number or something."

Robin's heart beat faster. She exchanged a look with Jerry. "Could it be a *formula* of some sort, Mr. Watson?"

Mr. Watson held it closer to his eyes. "It could, at that." He took the pitcher over to his desk. "Would you like me to write it down clearly for you?"

"Oh, yes, *please!*"

It took him a few minutes, and some frowning. Then he looked at the paper, nodding. "That seems to be it. It's new to me, but I'd say it's a formula for some sort of glaze."

Robin thanked him again. Her hand shook as she took the paper. She hoped he wouldn't guess what it was! The sooner she and Jerry got away from here, the better.

When they told Betty their story, she was almost as excited as they were. "You outdid yourself this time, Robin," she said. "That formula is really worth finding!"

"From what Jon said when he broke the blue bowl, the formula is worth a small fortune," Jerry reminded them. "And Robin ought to get the money!"

Betty considered. "But the formula belongs to Caleb's brother. The Gordons may know where he is. It might be best to put it in the bank for safekeeping, until they get back." She added, "If the formula is sold, I'm sure Robin will get some of the money."

Robin laughed. "Thanks, but no thanks!

Daddy would make me use it for college—and I'm not sure I'm wild about the idea of going to college. Unless—unless it's a *police college!*"

Robin and Jerry had several outings after that. Jason and Lucinda took them out some evenings. The most fun was a local fair with a Ferris wheel. But, much as she liked Jason and Lucinda, Robin privately felt that she had more fun alone with Jerry.

At the end of the week, as they were having supper, the telephone rang. Betty answered it, sounding surprised. "It's your father, Robin! They're back!" She held out the receiver and Robin took it.

"Daddy! How nice!" Robin cried. "But how come you're back so soon?"

"Things went much faster than we expected," Mr. Green said. "We got some fine offers for the land, and we've left a good lawyer in charge of everything. We'll tell you all about it when we see you."

Robin's mother came to the telephone then.

174

"Robin, darling!" she said. "We've missed you! You can come home any time you like— if Betty can spare you."

"Oh, she can," Robin said. "But I rather hate to leave Jerry Sands. He's a new friend of mine, and I sort of thought we'd both be here until school starts."

"Bring Jerry home with you for a visit," her mother said. "I'll telephone his mother if you'll give me the number."

But Robin wasn't sure what to do. "The trouble is, our town's so *boring*. Nothing ever happens. And Jerry's like me, he loves excitement."

Mrs. Green laughed. "I'm sure you'll find things to do. Even here. As a matter of fact, there's something new in town."

Robin was too eager to tell about her new plan to pay attention to what her mother had said.

"I suppose I could start getting ready for police college," Robin said. "I've decided that's where I'm going, when I finish high school. And Jerry might come, too." I'll put that idea into his head, she thought.

"Police college?" her mother said faintly. "Am I hearing right?"

Robin laughed. "You certainly are. But I have to finish high school first. I'll tell you and Daddy all about it when I get home." And she said good-bye and hung up, smiling from ear to ear, to offer her mother's invitation to Jerry.